To

for his grandchildren,

The Hammer of Thor

with kindest regards,

from,

Marvin Kendall.

Twelfth Night 2013.

Enjoy the Read!

The Hammer of Thor

Martin D. Kendall

Copyright © 2010 by Martin D. Kendall.

ISBN: Softcover   978-1-4568-1995-8
           Ebook   978-1-4568-1996-5

All rights reserved. No part of this book may be reproduced or transmitted in any form or by any means, electronic or mechanical, including photocopying, recording, or by any information storage and retrieval system, without permission in writing from the copyright owner.

This is a work of fiction. Names, characters, places and incidents either are the product of the author's imagination or are used fictitiously, and any resemblance to any actual persons, living or dead, events, or locales is entirely coincidental.

This book was printed in the United States of America.

To order additional copies of this book, contact:
Xlibris Corporation
0-800-644-6988
www.xlibrispublishing.co.uk
Orders@xlibrispublishing.co.uk

Contents

Preface 7

Chapter Null:	In the Beginning	9
Chapter One:	Arrival at Ilkley	11
Chapter Two:	The Swastika Stone and Wharfedale	19
Chapter Three:	A Strange Encounter in the Night	31
Chapter Four:	A Rainy Saturday	36
Chapter Five:	The Cow and Calf	44
Chapter Six:	The Badger Stone	54
Chapter Seven:	The Doubler Stones	62
Chapter Eight:	The Twelve Apostles	74
Chapter Nine:	The Badger Stone Revisited	86
Chapter Ten:	A Meeting with Thor	93
Chapter Eleven:	An Adventure in the Town Hall	98
Chapter Twelve:	The Journey to Almscliff	104
Chapter Thirteen:	The Giant Walks	109
Chapter Fourteen:	Aftermath	115

PREFACE

The background to the writing of this novel should be explained.

Upon being made redundant, while returning home to Ilkley, in a van with all my things in it, the idea for this novel was hatched. My friend, who was driving the van, happened to mention that another name for the Swastika pattern is The Hammer of Thor. He also hit on the idea of a cup and ring being involved.

The novel was written flat out in seven and a half weeks, and then several months were spent revising it in the light of friends' comments. Having thought of the riddles, the novel seemed to write itself around them.

It was set in a hypothetical 1994, during a Second Gulf War, hence the petrol rationing. Also many of the mental hospitals were due to close about then. Also not realising that, in fact, the date 7 September does not occur on a Thursday until 1995.

It should be noted that this was 1993, and this was pre-Internet and pre-mobile phones. Even the first Windows operating system did not come about until 1995. The world has changed out of all recognition since then, as has Ilkley.

For instance, the Station Plaza building was largely unoccupied. Now there are many shops, restaurants, a café, and the post office in it.

In those innocent days, the children's grandparents, Len and Molly, would have had no qualms about letting the children out unattended on the Moor. They are also largely unafraid of the strange man, Jim, they meet on the Moor. They would be much more wary these days.

The conditions at White Wells were very rudimentary, then. The only source of energy was bottled gas, and the lighting was via gas mantles for the couple that lived there. Since then, a pipeline has been brought in with all the utilities in it.

There was some research done about metal detecting, but it was not discovered that metal detecting in the Aire and Wharfe valleys is strictly governed by the Two Dales Metal Detecting Club. People like Joe Grimshaw simply do not exist, or, if they do, they should be deplored.

Also, in the seventeen years since writing the novel, both, The Captain and Jim, have passed away.

It will be found that the boy in the novel tends to rather domineer the poor girl. Apologies for that, it was just the way the story came out. There are certain other details that do not seem to entirely ring true that had to be adopted for the sake of the story.

All that having been said, it starts slowly, then builds up to a climax at the end. Enjoy the Read!

Martin Kendall 2010.

CHAPTER NULL

In the Beginning

The Moor had secrets in its heart it would tell no man. The old stones kept the secrets. Impenetrable. Immovable. They knew the time was near. There was an air of expectancy in the whistle of the wind in the heather and in the sullen silences. They were coming soon.

The Moor was waiting.

The Moor was waiting.

CHAPTER ONE

Arrival at Ilkley

With a clattering noise, the train rounded the corner, and a vista of Ilkley Moor was revealed to the two children.

'That must be the Cow and Calf, Ginny!' Arthur called out. There was a tall cliff looming high up on their left with a huge boulder in front of it. The bracken on the Moor was beginning to turn brown in the late summer. The sun shone down as the train clanked its way the remaining mile or so to Ilkley station. The town was bathed in sunshine, making the drab, grey roofs look friendly.

Finally, with a note of resignation, the train pulled in, screeching to a halt. The children grabbed their bags and stepped off on to the platform. A tannoy crackled to life.

'European Rail would like to apologise for the late arrival of the 16.38 from Leeds', announced a voice. 'This was due to a cow on the line at Burley-in-Wharfedale.'

'I suppose it was the wrong sort of cow!' muttered Arthur.

At first the children could not get their bearings.

'I think, it's this way,' said Ginny. They hurried along the platform, lugging their bags after them.

'Oh! Where are they!' cried Ginny. 'I don't even know what they look like!'

But they need not have worried. There, at the end of the platform, stood a figure as sturdy as the Cow Rock and with a smile as broad as the Yorkshire Dales. He was dressed in a tweed suit and had a cardigan on, even though the weather was hot. He was wearing a flat cap.

'Oh! There you are, Grandad!' said Ginny, giving him a peck on the cheek. 'We thought we had lost you!'

'Leonard's the name, boot you can call me Len,' said Leonard Dickinson. 'And what's the 'oorry? We 'ave all t' time in t' world oop 'ere. Molly is waitin' in t' trap outside. I'll teck your bags.'

They made their way through the entrance hall, the white walls of which were marred by graffiti. A horse and a brightly coloured trap were waiting in the car park. Molly Dickinson was in the trap. Molly had a flowery hat on and clutched a handbag in her lap. She gave both the children a kiss.

'Well, now', said Molly, 'you moost be Arthur and you moost be Guinevere. If you don't look exactly like your Mum and Dad.'

'Please call me Ginny,' said Ginny. 'I hate being called Guinevere. If only Dad had not been so taken up with King Arthur.'

'Ginny it shall be, then.' Molly laughed. 'Climb aboard. We're not bothered by t' petrol rationin' as you can see.'

The children climbed up behind Molly. Leonard hoisted the bags into the back of the trap, climbed up beside Molly, and with a 'Gee up, Bracken,' they set off.

They set off to the west on to the main street. Molly held her hat to her head.

'No doubt you've already seen t' Cow and Calf, but I'll point out soom of t' things as we go along,' shouted Leonard above the noise of the wheels and the clip-clop of Bracken. 'If you joost look oop on t' Moor to the left now, you'll see White Wells.'

High up on the Moor, the children could make out a set of cottages, which were indeed painted bright white.

'And this is t' Grove.'

They were passing down a wide, tree-lined avenue. The shops lining the Grove, however, were a sorry sight. Many of them were boarded up, and there was a general air of dilapidation.

'Those shops . . . I suppose it's the Middle East War and the petrol rationing, Len,' said Arthur.

'Aye,' said Leonard. 'We don't get as many tourists 'ere as we used to.'

'How do people get to work from here?' asked Arthur.

'Trains and booses,' said Leonard. 'They've 'ad to lay on extra trains at peak times to Leeds and Bratford. Soom people work from 'oom with computers, you know. That is, them as 'as work.'

They were now going uphill, past many big houses with extensive grounds. Finally, they came to a large wood with a babbling beck.

'This, 'ere, is Heber's Ghyll,' said Leonard. 'The Heber family used to own this land. Bishop Heber wrote several famous hymns.'

They swung through an open gate, went up a short, rising track, and came into a farmyard. 'And 'ere we are! Folfoot Farm! Your 'oom for t' present,' exclaimed Leonard, jumping down from the trap. A sheepdog raced up to meet him.

'Now, down, Jess!' commanded Leonard. The children got out of the trap, looking all around, and Jess proceeded to make a fuss of them.

'I said, down, Jess,' Leonard commanded again. 'She's not used to strangers. Soomtimes, in winter, she sees no one at all. She'll get used to you in time.'

Folfoot Farm was not big but was well laid. There was a main farmhouse, partly covered in ivy. It was made of the local golden-coloured sandstone, which is called 'Millstone Grit'. It looked very old. Opposite were a stable and a shippon attached to it. The cattle in the shippon had been disturbed and were bellowing from it. The farmyard was cobbled. The farm buildings ran east-west. To the north, Ilkley valley lay spread out before them with the peak of Beamsley Beacon visible on the far side. To the south, the ground rose steeply to Ilkley Moor, where some small crags could be seen.

While Leonard was leading Bracken to the stable, Molly was showing the children into the farmhouse. They could not help noticing the inscription, TO KNOW THYSELF IS A PROOF OF WISDOM, LD, 1652, over the main door. There was a mounting block for getting on to horses against the front wall. The children were led inside, where there was a short entrance hall. Molly hung up their coats and her hat on some pegs. There was a stone-flagged kitchen to the right and a living room to the left. Straight ahead were steps leading upstairs. Molly chivvied them into the living room.

'Sit thisen down,' said Molly. 'You'll be wantin' soom tea and soom cake?'

'That'd be fine, Molly,' said Ginny.

The children collapsed into battered armchairs of uncertain vintage and looked around, while Molly retired to the kitchen. There was a dresser behind them with some very old-looking pieces of china on it, a dark oak sideboard with various mementoes and framed photographs on it, a table with a checked tablecloth spread over it, a grandfather clock in the corner ticking the time away, and, dominating the room, an inglenook fireplace. The fire was not made, the weather being very hot. They noticed that in the front face of the mantelpiece were inscribed the letters LD and the date, 1652. A ginger cat was asleep in a basket by the fireplace. They noticed that there was no television set in sight, only a battered old radio set.

Molly bustled back into the room with a tray just as Leonard came in through the front door, stamping his boots and carrying the children's bags.

Molly handed two plates to the children and poured them tea in two bone china cups. The children tucked in gratefully.

'Don't eat too mooch. We'll be 'avin' soopper soon,' warned Molly.

Leonard came into the living room, having taken the children's bags upstairs.

'Looks like there's a storm brewin',' said Leonard. 'I thought as 'ow it were a bit close.'

At that point, there was a big gust of wind. Some soot fell down the chimney and the windows rattled.

'Appen I'll go out agen and check t' farm,' said Leonard and proceeded to go back to the corridor and put on his boots, before going out of the front door.

'Well, now', said Molly, 'you moost be tired after your journey.'

'Not too tired, are we, Ginny?' answered Arthur. Ginny shook her head.

'Well, then, tell me about my daughter and 'er 'usband. 'Ow is David doin' out in the Middle East?'

'Since Dad was called up, he's been flying all over. We're very worried about him. It's very dangerous where he is. As you know, Mum couldn't cope with us alone. It's very good of you to agree to have us here at such short notice.'

'Well, that's what we're 'ere for, to take you in, in our daughter's hour of need. What else can a mother and father do for their daughter?'

'It's very kind of you, Molly.'

'I won't 'ear anoother word about it while you're 'ere. Now it's about six o'clock, and soopper'll be at seven.'

As if to prove it, the grandfather clock in the corner chimed six times. Arthur glanced at his digital watch. The clock was about five minutes slow. By this time, the rain was rattling on the windows. The children felt warm and safe inside. Molly had popped back into the kitchen. She came back into the living room.

'I'm joost mekin' t' soopper. I'll be in t' kitchen, if you want me. We don't 'ave any televisions at this farm. Leonard can't abide them. There's a radio 'ere. T' valves take soom time to warm up. There are soom magazines and books next to t' radio, and there's a pack o' cards in t' sideboard.'

'I'm sure we'll be OK,' said Ginny. 'We don't like television much, anyway. All those repeats, soaps, and moronic game shows.'

Molly collected the tray and retreated to the kitchen, from where there could be heard the occasional clatter of pots and pans. Arthur got up and fiddled with the radio. There were all sorts of strange stations marked on it such as Hilversum, which, Arthur realised, probably no longer existed. Meanwhile, Ginny was looking at some of the old books and the framed paintings on the wall. There were sepia photographs of men in stovepipe hats and women in crinolines. They all looked very dour, as they were not smiling. Ginny was amused by one book by a Stackpool E. O'Dell, which was about phrenology, the old science of the shape of the head. It had a diagram in the front, which tried to link intelligence to the slant of the nose. Arthur flicked through some farming magazines. He found that the references in them to AI were not to artificial intelligence, as he had at first thought, but to artificial insemination.

Eventually, Leonard came back in, very wet, having forgotten his waterproofs. Molly heard him and fussed around him like an old mother hen. She gave him a change of some of his outer clothing.

Leonard came into the living room, turning on the light. It was getting quite dark.

'There's nowt wrong that won't wait while t' mornin'.'

Molly came in, set the table, and then shepherded them to it. The meal was not too big, but everyone felt full by the time it was finished. Molly cleared the table and retired to the kitchen. The children offered to help with the washing-up, but Molly explained that she preferred to be left alone in her kitchen. The clock chimed eight. Arthur went over to the radio.

'Could we just listen to the news?' he asked Leonard. 'I want to hear how the Middle East War is going.'

Arthur turned on the radio. The speaker gave out a complaining noise. Arthur fiddled with the dial and then they heard,

'. . . second day of heavy casualties. It is reported that two RAF fighter jets were shot down in the Hakron desert this afternoon. Most of the crew members were rescued by UN forces, but there are still two pilots missing . . . . Now the sports news . . . Leeds United drew one all with Manchester United today at . . .'

Arthur turned off the radio.

'I hope that's not Dad,' he said, looking worried.

'Oh, nivver you mind,' said Leonard. 'Your Dad can look after 'issen.'

Arthur went back and sat down at the table, still looking worried.

'It's coom over awl coold, like,' said Leonard. 'I'll light t' fire.'

He proceeded to take some logs out of a basket by the fire. The cat was disturbed and it moved itself haughtily over to the settee, flopped down, and went to sleep, seemingly in one movement. Leonard screwed up some old newspapers, laid them under the logs, set light to them, and soon had a blaze going.

Molly came back in, drew the curtains, and they were all seated around the fire.

'I've been wondering about the initials over the fireplace and the front door,' mused Arthur.

'You tell 'im, Father,' said Molly.

'That'll be my goodness knows 'ow many times great grandfather, Leonard Dickinson,' answered Leonard. 'There's bin a Dickinson at Folfoot Farm for over three 'undred years. Unfortunately, there was no son in my generation.'

'My mother . . .'

'Aye, we only 'ad one daughter, and now she's down south. Poor Molly, 'ere, near died in childbirth producin' 'er. We weren't about to 'ave anoother child.'

'So that's why she's called Leonora!'

'What else could you call your only daughter when she cooms from such ancestors? 'Ow is she, anyway?'

'You know she can't dance any more. Her arthritis is too bad. That's why she can't look after us without Dad helping.'

'And 'er a professional dancer, an' all!'

Leonard clicked his tongue. There was a silence. The fire crackled and spat sparks up the chimney.

'Tell me about the Moor,' said Arthur, breaking the silence.

'It's a very strange place. Mists blow up from nowhere. Gives me the willies soomtimes, and I've bin farmin' 'ere all me life.'

At that point, there was a gigantic peal of thunder. It seemed to be right overhead. The children jumped a little.

'It's all reet,' said Leonard. 'We've 'ad worse than this afore and weathered it. I'll tell you what, now that we're all gathered round t' fire, I'll tell you t' old stories that my father toold me when I were a lad. Turn t' light out, Moother.'

Molly turned the light out. Leonard took an old briar pipe from the mantelshelf and a pouch of tobacco from his pocket. He made a great play of tamping down the tobacco and lighting the pipe, enjoying the atmosphere. Then, with his craggy face lit only by the firelight, the tobacco glowing in the bowl, and the thunder pealing overhead, Leonard proceeded to tell the following tale:

There once was a giant. Giant Rombald was his name and the whole Moor is now named after him. Well, one morning, he was walking from Almscliff Crag over to the Cow Rock. Almscliff Crag is a large outcrop about ten miles east down Wharfedale. Anyhow, when he got to the Cow Rock, he tripped over it and broke off the Calf. There is a hollow in the top of the Cow Rock that is known as the Giant's Footprint. The giant's wife, who was gathering stones in her skirt, some say to throw at the giant after an argument, came running across the Moor. In her haste, she dropped her skirtful of stones on the Moor. And that is how the Calf broke off the Cow and still, to this day, there is a pile of stones on the Moor, called the Skirtful of Stones.

'And there's an old family rhyme that's bin in our family for generations', said Leonard, 'about the giant. It goes summat like this,

> *One, Two, Three, Four,*
> *The Stones they stand upon the Moor,*
> *The Hammer it is lost to Thor,*
> *They all await the Maiden pure.*
>
> *Find thou the Cup and find thou the Ring,*
> *The Cup that, from which, drank the King,*
> *The Ring of which the Minstrels sing,*
> *Both to the Badger thou must bring.*
>
> *The Giant at the Dawn shall walk,*
> *To Almscliff from the Vale of York,*
> *Then fly as high as any Hawk,*
> *To the Moor of which the Legend talks.*
>
> *One, Two, Three, Four,*
> *The Stones they stand upon the Moor,*
> *The Hammer it is lost to Thor,*
> *They all await the Maiden pure.*

'That's 'ow my father told me, and 'is father told 'im,' said Leonard. 'Goodness only knows what t' rhyme means.'

The children applauded.

The clock struck ten thirty. The cat yawned and stretched and ran off into the kitchen to find some food.

'I could tell you mooch more about t' Moor. About t' old stones and t' Druids', said Leonard, 'though I allus say as 'ow off-comedens know more than I do. However, I can see by t' way you're yawning and by t' time on t' clock that we should all be in bed.'

Leonard switched the lights on again. The children blinked sleepily in the light. Molly immediately led them up to their room. She opened the door to it and then turned towards Arthur and Ginny.

'You don't mind sharin' a room together?' she asked them. 'It's all we've got for you.'

'Not at all, do we, Arthur?' said Ginny, looking at him.

'Oh, no,' returned Arthur, 'we're used to moving around and sharing rooms.'

Molly led them into the bedroom. There were two beds and an old washstand with a white pitcher and bowl on it. The beds were covered by counterpanes made of squares of brightly coloured knitted wool.

'Owd Granny Dickinson knitted these counterpanes,' said Molly, lovingly running her hand over them. 'Though she were eighty-two at t' time and 'alf-blind. The bathroom's 'ere to the left of me. Well, I'll love you and leave you now. Sleep well!'

The storm was still raging. The children could not resist peering around the curtains at the Moor. The lightning was flickering over the crags. Ginny screwed up her eyes.

'I think there's someone on that rock up there, Arthur,' said Ginny.

'Don't be silly, Ginny. Who'd be on the Moor at this time of night and in this weather? It's a trick of the light,' said Arthur.

'I still think I can see someone,' reiterated Ginny.

'Perhaps it's the lightning conductor!' joshed Arthur.

Ginny pushed Arthur's shoulder in mock anger.

The children were soon in bed and soon fell fast asleep. They hardly noticed when the storm finally abated. Both children's dreams were a strange mixture of the Cow and Calf, giants, and rocks tumbling out of the sky.

CHAPTER TWO

The Swastika Stone and Wharfedale

As the last of the night creatures returned to their burrows and roosts, the first rays of the sun were fingering the edges of the curtains at Folfoot Farm. The day promised to be bright, slightly breezy, and fresh.

The children woke early, but not early enough to wake the Dickinsons. When the children had got dressed, sorted out some of the things in their bags, and gone downstairs, Leonard was long gone, seeing to something on the farm, they suspected. Molly was already well into her day's tasks. She liked to get on early with her baking. The fire was still smouldering from the previous night.

'Good mornin', Arthur and Ginny, did you sleep well?' asked Molly.

'Like tops!' chorused the children.

'Then you'll be wantin' breakfast?' asked Molly. 'We can't afford it all t' time, but would you like a proper, old-English breakfast? I've got eggs, bacon, and black puddin'. It won't teck a moment.'

Arthur looked at Ginny.

'We would rather just have cereal and toast, Molly,' said Arthur.

Molly looked disappointed.

'You're growin' young things,' said Molly. 'You need your energy.'

'All the same, we would much rather have a light breakfast, Molly,' apologised Ginny.

'Very well, then,' said Molly. 'That's what you shall 'ave. Sit thisen down at t' table. Do you want tea or coffee?'

'I have coffee, and Ginny, here, has tea. Neither of us takes sugar,' explained Arthur.

Molly fussed off into the kitchen and soon brought out some butter and home-made marmalade. In a while, she brought out a mug of coffee, an earthenware pot of tea, some milk in a blue jug, some packs of cereal, and an embarrassment of toast. The sun was shining through the window as the children had their breakfast. It glinted through the marmalade, just as it did in all the adverts. The children could not finish the toast and had to leave half of it.

'You eat like birds,' commented Molly when she saw that. 'I don't know what young bairns are coomin' to.'

'It's just the modern way,' replied Arthur. 'Incidentally, we're thinking of going up on the Moor this morning.'

'You go and get ready, and then I'll talk to you about it,' said Molly.

The children made their way upstairs, washed, and got out their walking gear. Ginny saw what Arthur was getting out.

'Not that old rucksack and horrible old Cagjack,' said Ginny, 'They both need washing. What's in that rucksack, anyway?'

'Mind your own business, Ginny,' said Arthur, pulling on his boots and hefting the rucksack.

At that moment, the children heard the phone ringing. Molly answered it. It was Leonora. Molly called Arthur and Ginny downstairs. They took turns talking to their mother, who had some bad news for them. She had been told that one of the pilots missing in the Hakron desert was their father. She told the children not to be concerned and that he would probably turn up soon. She asked the children how they were. They told her that they had arrived safely and the things they intended to do. Wishing their mother well, they put the phone down.

'Well, we'll just have to keep our fingers crossed,' commented Arthur to Ginny.

Molly had heard the telephone conversation.

'Now, children,' she said, 'don't you go spoilin' your day by woorryin' about your father. Promise me you won't.'

Arthur and Ginny said that they would wait until some more definite news came through. Meanwhile, they were still going up on the Moor.

'Me and Len were wonderin' about lettin' you out alone on t' Moor,' said Molly. 'But I suppose you're old enough. Mind you, don't talk to any strange men and keep to t' tracks. 'Ere's a two-and-a-'alf inch map of t' Moor and a town plan of Ilkley. Try and be back by twelve and mind you look out for any grouse shootin' oop there. Len thought as 'ow he might teck you oop t' Wharfe this afternoon. Off you go!'

Arthur said that they would look after themselves and could they have a flask of hot water to make some tea. He packed it in his bag, and they set out. On stepping out of the front door, a flock of hens came up nervously, having been used to being fed scraps by Molly. They scattered when the children moved forward, Arthur inspecting the map of Ilkley Moor.

'There's a path going up on to the Moor here,' said Arthur, pointing at the map. 'And there's something called the Swastika Stone marked here. Let's go and have a look.'

As the children set off across the fields, rabbits scattered into holes known only to them. Bejewelled cobwebs hung between the stalks of plants. Wood pigeons cooed from the nearby wood, and there were cattle lowing in the fields.

'Are they Friesian, Ginny?' said Arthur, pointing at the cows.

'Of course they are, Arthur,' replied Ginny.

'I thought they would be "Friesian" up here!' smirked Arthur.

'Why can't you tell me some "udder" joke!' retorted Ginny, giving as good as she got. 'You're a loony, you know that, Arthur?'

'I was in a mental hospital, once, remember?' replied Arthur.

'I don't want to talk about that,' said Ginny, crossly. 'You tell people all about it at the drop of a hat.'

As they got higher, the dying bracken, still wet from the night's rain, brushed against their jeans, making them quite wet. They came up a gully between two outcrops and turned eastward along the top. The wind was much fresher here. Skylarks were playing overhead. They were following a drystone wall of millstone grit at the edge of the rise, where there were ruins of long-abandoned buildings. The wind whistled eerily past the branches of some stunted Scotch pines. They climbed over a stile and were on the open edge. Presently, they came to an outcrop with an iron railing and barbed wire all around it.

'This looks like the Swastika Stone,' said Arthur.

'I think this is where I saw someone last night,' said Ginny.

Arthur shrugged. Both the children looked through the railings. They saw a stone in the grass with a carving on it like this:

'It doesn't look anything like the Nazi Swastika,' said Ginny. 'Anyway, I think that goes around the other way.'

'Wait a minute, Ginny!' exclaimed Arthur. 'I think that's only an illustration. Look out on the large rock there. Can't you see something faint?'

Through the railings, they saw, the same marking, which was very faint.

'I wonder how old that is. It looks very old,' said Ginny.

'Perhaps we can find out in town,' said Arthur.

'Hang on a minute. I am feeling thirsty. Can't we just stop for five minutes, Arthur?' queried Ginny.

'What, already? We've only just started!' complained Arthur.

'Can't we stop? It's such a lovely day,' pleaded Ginny.

'Oh, all right, but we can't stop for long or drink much. We've got to be back by twelve, and this is only a small flask,' conceded Arthur.

They sat down on some stones next to the railing. Arthur rummaged in his rucksack and brought out the flask and some dried milk. He rummaged in his bag again.

'Damn! I've forgotten the tea bags,' said Arthur.

'Then we'll just have to have Ilkley Moor tea,' said Ginny.

'What's Ilkley Moor tea?' asked Arthur.

'Hot water with dried milk, silly!' chuckled Ginny.

Arthur made up two cups, and the children surveyed the scene, Arthur looking at the map. In front of them and to the south, there was a short boggy plateau, after which the Moor rose to another ridge, beyond which they could not see. To their left and to the east, a vast swathe of the Moor in green, purple, and brown was revealed, with a distant view of the Cow Rock. Suddenly, Arthur pointed.

'Can you see? Just on the horizon, I think that's Almscliff Crag!' he exclaimed.

They could see a faint shape silhouetted against the horizon to the east.

'Maybe not. I don't know. The map doesn't go that far,' retracted Arthur.

The children got up and looked along the Wharfe valley. To the north-west they could see Addingham and the bypass. A year ago, the bypass would have been streaming with traffic, but now it was deserted. They could also make out the broad curve of the Wharfe as it turned north, and was obscured by Beamsley Beacon.

Spread below them to the north-east was the whole of Ilkley. A gasometer interrupted the broad spread of the grey and red rooftops. They could see a spire in the centre of the town.

'Is that spire the parish church, Arthur?' queried Ginny.

'I think that spire's Christ Church. You can see a church nearer the river. That's All Saints' Church. That's the parish church,' answered Arthur.

'We had better be off. It's nearly nine thirty,' said Arthur. 'There's Heber's Ghyll over here. Let's go down it.'

Arthur packed up. The wind sounded in the neck of the flask as he re-screwed the cap. A little spider let itself down from the flask on a silver thread.

The children set off eastward. Soon they were in amongst the bracken and were descending. Eventually, they arrived at a point where there was a bridge over the beck to the right and a small iron gate ahead. Through the gate was a wood. They let themselves through the gate and descended Heber's Ghyll. The vegetation was lush and the atmosphere humid. The sunlight was dappled in the wood. They counted six rustic bridges as they went down, criss-crossing the Ghyll. In the beck were moss-covered stones, and ferns draped the banks. The beck splashed hurriedly over the stones. At the bottom, they crossed over a final bridge and came out on to the road.

'Let's go back to Folfoot Farm, Arthur,' suggested Ginny.

'No,' said Arthur, 'we've still got some time yet. Let's go into town. Firstly, I've seen St Margaret's Church on the map. I'd like to see that.'

Ginny reluctantly agreed, and they climbed a set of steps near the road and started downhill. Presently, they came to the church, but it was locked. They went over the road and set off again.

'Hello! What's this!' exclaimed Ginny.

They looked through an opening in the hedge on the left and saw some stones surrounded by a green-painted railing. They stepped into an area surrounded by trees. There was a notice behind the railing. It read.

These boulders were decorated in the Bronze Age, 3,500 years ago. They were originally located in the Panorama Woods but were moved to their present site in 1892.

'Three thousand, five hundred years!' breathed Arthur, 'Those markings are old!'

The stones were very weathered, but the children could make out some strange markings on them. Just then, there was a movement behind them, and they turned to find a tall, helmeted Policeman staring down at them.

'And what are you kids doing here?' said the Police Officer. 'Up to mischief, I'll be bound!'

'We're just looking around, Officer. We're new to this area,' said Arthur defensively.

'And you've come to look at the stones?' questioned the Officer.

'That's right,' said Arthur, still on his guard.

'Well, I'll tell you something. I wouldn't walk past this place at night, and I'm not afraid of much,' intoned the Officer, 'Well, I've got much more important things to do than talk to you all day. Remember, I'll be keeping my eye on you two.'

With that, the Officer swept out of the area, and they heard the sound of a car driving away.

'He wasn't very pleasant, was he?' commented Ginny.

The children set off into town again. On reaching the shopping area, they noticed that there were not many people around, it being a weekday. When they reached the Grove, they decided that they did not like the run-down atmosphere, so they turned off into a street on the left. Here, there was an ironmonger's. It looked reasonably prosperous. They noticed that the windows were full of all sorts of gadgets and gimmicks for the home. There were place mats, steam irons, gas cylinders, and even lawnmowers.

'I suppose that they supply the local farmers,' Arthur thought to himself.

They carried on to what they realised was the oldest part of the town. Rounding a corner into Church Street, there was a view of a picturesque collection of old buildings, all in the local stone. They gathered that there had been several restaurants and cafes here at one time, but only a few were still open. There was a Victorian arcade, which they nosed around. They then crossed over the street and, up a bit from an old pub with a sundial, they found an archway with the sign Art Gallery and Museum over it. Through the tunnel-like entrance, they found a cobbled courtyard and an old building with mullioned windows. A lavender flowerbed was buzzing with bees. They guessed that the building was the old manor house. They tried the studded door, but it was locked.

'Everything's locked around here!' complained Ginny.

They turned around and climbed a short flight of steps up to the All Saints Church. They walked around the corner, past several old gravestones, and into the porch of the church.

'At least something's open,' said Arthur.

They spent a while looking at the various notices in the porch. The notices were generally about world poverty. They then turned the iron ring in the inner door, and it opened. Inside, they found a printed guide to the church, and put the money for the guide into a slot marked BOOKS in the wall. Nearby, they came upon three Saxon crosses, two of which were headless. The diagrams on the wall explained the symbols on the crosses. There were symbols for Mark, Matthew, Luke, and John and a pattern depicting the world tree with a serpent at the base. Alongside the crosses were the remains of some Roman altars.

A lady was arranging flowers. She saw the children and introduced herself as Madeleine English. She was a tall lady in her late fifties with greying hair. She was wearing a twinset and pearls and looked like an outdoor type. Madeleine found out that the children were new to the area and offered to show them around. Firstly, they saw a font with a heavy wooden cover. The wooden cover could be raised with a rope over a pulley. Secondly, they were led to an intricately carved, wooden pulpit. Lastly, they saw a interesting figure of a medieval knight reclining cross-legged. There were beautiful stained-glass windows, and they noticed that all the hassocks were embroidered with various motifs. They learnt that the All Saints' Church was built on the site of a Roman fort. The fort was named Olicana. Thanking Madeleine, who asked them if they would like to come to a service there on Sunday, the children stepped out into the daylight outside the porch.

Arthur and Ginny inspected their watches. It was about eleven o'clock. They estimated it would take them half an hour to get back to Folfoot Farm. Again, Ginny was for going back, but Arthur wanted to explore still further. Arthur dragged Ginny down to some riverside gardens, where they stopped on a bench in a play area and had some more Ilkley Moor tea. There were nannies and mothers watching their children play. One nanny was trying to coax a child off a slide in order to go home. The child would not do anything it was told and was sulking.

'I wouldn't like that job,' Ginny whispered to Arthur.

The children visited an old packhorse bridge, then, finally, had a hot, dusty walk to the outskirts of the town, and went back to Folfoot Farm. They were using a route that Arthur had worked out from the town plan.

They were late by half an hour in arriving back at the farm. They were footsore and gagging for a drink.

From her kitchen, Molly had heard the tramp of their boots on the cobbles. She was waiting at the door.

'We're sorry we're a bit late, Molly,' apologised Ginny.

'Oh, you don't want to go woorryin' about that,' said Molly. 'We work on a different clock oop here. Now, Len'll be back from Addingham Moorside soon. But, first, you'll be wantin' your lunch. I teck it, knowin' you, that you'll be wantin' a light one?'

'Yes, please,' said Ginny.

'Well, then, coom in and teck off your boots. You look fair worn out,' said Molly.

The children crowded into the hall, dragged off their boots, and collapsed into the armchairs in the living room. From the depths of her kitchen, Molly was asking the children all about the morning's adventures. They tried to explain where they had been as Molly commented on it. When they told her about the church and the woman who had shown them around, Molly said that she knew her. Everyone seemed to know everyone else in Ilkley. 'Not like down south', the children thought, 'where everyone kept themselves to themselves'. In a short while, they had drinks in their hands, and a while later, they were seated at the table for lunch.

Molly was trying very hard to match her meals to the children's appetites, but still there was more than they could handle. There was home-made bread, still slightly warm, cheese, pickle, tomatoes, beetroot, and lettuce, and for afters there was a gooseberry pie. Leonard came in while the children were still eating.

'Ello, there, Ginny and Arthur,' he said. 'I've been thinkin' of teckin' you oop t' Wharfe to Burnsall, this afternoon. That is, if you still want to go.'

'Yes, please, Len!' the children said in unison.

'Aren't you having any lunch?' asked Arthur.

'I allus 'as sandwiches when I'm out on t' farm. Molly mecks me them,' said Leonard.

After finishing their meal, the children got themselves ready to go. They put on lighter shoes. Arthur decided to put his boots away in a cupboard in the hall. He opened the door. He was just about to put his boots away when he spotted a vicious-looking knife on a shelf. He picked it up. It had weird carvings all over it.

'What's this knife?' he asked Leonard.

Leonard grabbed the knife from Arthur and shoved it quickly back in the cupboard, closing the door.

'Leave that alone!' he exclaimed. 'We don't want you playin' with knives.'

'But what's it for?' asked Arthur.

Leonard looked embarrassed.

'Oh, I use it for gettin' t' rot out of t' sheep's feet,' he explained. 'Don't go back in that cupboard agen.'

Arthur was puzzled but asked no further questions. Leonard went out to the stable to get Bracken.

Finally, Arthur and Ginny joined Leonard in the farmyard with the trap. Molly was staying at home. Soon they were trundling down the same way that they had found back to the farm.

As they were going along the Addingham road, Arthur was wondering about the markings on the rocks.

'Tell me about the old stones on the Moor, Len?' Arthur asked Leonard.

'T' markings on them are known as cup and ring marks, Arthur,' said Leonard. 'All I know is that they are very old. Some say as 'ow they were put there by t' Druids. If you want to explore on t' Moor, you'll 'ave to go oop by thisen. I've got enough work to do on t' farm. Remember that you start at Ilkley Grammar a week on Monday. You won't 'ave mooch time to explore on t' Moor then.'

'Yes, we know that. What do you know about the original Leonard Dickinson?' Arthur continued.

'Some say as 'ow 'e were the last of t' Druids,' said Leonard. 'Any road 'e were a wise man and soothsayer. 'E once said,

When iron floats on water,
And iron flies in air,
Horseless carriages will ride,
And, then, thou best beware.

'Which came true, as you know.

'It is also said that 'e made a pact with t' Devil, who lost, and built Folfoot Farm as a forfeit. They say as 'ow 'is ghost still haunts t' farm. I've seen summat out of t' corner of my eye a few times, late at neet. Fair put t' wind oop me.'

The sun went behind a cloud. Leonard's face had turned thoughtful. The crags over the Moor looked dark. Bracken had stopped.

Suddenly, a low-flying jet fighter screamed overhead and then thundered on up the Wharfe valley. Bracken reared up. Leonard brought him quickly under control and waved his fist in the air at the retreating fighter.

'Flipping jets!' he cursed. 'I 'ate 'em.'

'Remember that our Dad is flying in one of those!' exclaimed Ginny.

'Ee! I'm sorry, lass. I spoke out o' turn,' apologised Leonard.

'Oh, I don't really mind,' said Ginny. 'What is that jet doing here?'

'They're allus practisin' low-flyin' oop t' Dales,' replied Leonard. 'No harm done. Let's be movin' on.'

The sun had come out again. Leonard started up Bracken with a click of the tongue and a shake of the reins. They travelled on through Addingham to Bolton Bridge, and were soon in the village of Bolton Abbey. The double yellow lines here seemed unnecessary as there was hardly anyone about. On visiting the Abbey buildings, Arthur and Ginny read some signs fixed to the wall. They discovered that the Abbey was incorrectly named, and should really have been called a Priory. The children found out that it had originally been a monastery of Augustinian canons called 'Black Canons'. It was a mostly a ruin now. They played 'ducks and drakes' for a while, skimming stones in the river. They also bought postcards at the little village post office and stores.

Travelling on, they came to The Strid. It took them some time to get down to the Wharfe, and the rocks were slippery. When they reached The Strid, they found a narrow gap in the Millstone Grit, through which the whole of the Wharfe thundered.

The Strid

The children discovered that it was called The Strid because it was only a stride across, but woe betide anyone who attempted to cross here! They noticed a big sign in red warning of the danger. Leonard mentioned a legend about the Boy of Egremond and that Wharfe means swift water. He also told the children that there was an old rhyme which went,

> *Wharfe is clear,*
> *And Aire is lithe,*
> *Where the Aire drowns one,*
> *The Wharfe drowns five.*

Continuing on their way, they next came upon a lovely ruin called Barden Tower. Leonard told them about the Shepherd Lord, who had lived here in Tudor times. On the ground floor, they could make out the ruins of a great hall and fireplace. They could imagine the feasting that went on there.

Finally, they came to Burnsall. Coming down the hill to it, they could see a tiny hamlet nestling in the valley with a magnificent bridge on piers over the Wharfe. When they got into the village, the children saw an old pub near the bridge and a large green next to the river. They visited the church, which had an interesting revolving lychgate, some Anglo-Saxon sculpture, and Viking hogback tombstones.

The children wanted to stop for a while, so Leonard bought them ice creams in the village store, and they sat on the green. The children wrote their postcards with a pen that Arthur always carried in the pocket of his Cagjack.

After enjoying the scenery for a while, Leonard took the children home the back way. They travelled along many highways and byways over a bridge and a ford and were always close to the Wharfe. They went back almost to Bolton Bridge, but they turned off and went through the village of Beamsley. At the end of the village, they turned up Beamsley Beacon and nearly went over it. Bracken slowed almost to a walking pace. On the far side, the children found a postbox near a farm and posted their cards.

They went back to Folfoot Farm via the centre of Ilkley, noticing how the Moor dominated the town. Molly was waiting at the farm.

'What do you think to Wharfedale, now?' asked Molly.

'It's marvellous!' said Ginny happily.

'I think you'd say "It's reet grand!"' said Arthur, laughing.

It seemed as if, in no time at all, the children had had their tea, gone upstairs to bed, and fallen asleep. That night, Arthur slept deeply and dreamlessly, but Ginny tossed and turned in her bed.

Burnsall, Wharfedale

CHAPTER THREE

A Strange Encounter in the Night

They were in a desert. The sun was beating mercilessly down, and her father was being chased by someone. It was the Officer that they had met at the old stones in town. He was dressed in an Arab's clothes and had a black pointed beard. Ginny was trying to head him off and protect her father. Suddenly, the Officer pulled out a gun and thrust it under Ginny's nose. He was pulling the trigger . . .

Ginny woke with a start. Ginger, the cat, was tickling her nose with his tail. He was asleep on her bed.

Ginny lay for a moment and then shook herself and wiped her eyes with the back of her hands. She turned on her bedside light as the nightmare faded in her mind. Ginny had become puzzled.

'That's strange', thought Ginny, 'Len and Molly don't normally allow Ginger upstairs.'

But that was not all. Rising and falling on the air, Ginny could hear some voices.

She looked at her watch. It was one o'clock in the morning. Ginny lay there and decided that she had better investigate. Maybe, she thought, it was burglars and the Police had better be called. She crawled out of her warm bed and put on a nightgown and slippers. She quietly opened the door to the bedroom. Ginger ran out of the room. Ginny tiptoed downstairs and opened the front door on to the cold, night air. She noticed that the door had been left unlocked. She could still hear voices. She went back upstairs to warn Len and Molly. She hesitantly knocked on their door.

'Len! Molly!' she called in a low voice.

There was no answer. She knocked harder. Still there was no answer. Finally, she swung the door open and looked in. By the rays of her bedside light spilling across the landing, she could not make out anyone in bed. She turned on the light. Len's and Molly's clothes were piled up to one side, but there was no one in the bed.

'Stranger and stranger,' Ginny thought.

Ginny now decided that she had to wake Arthur. She went back to their bedroom, went over to Arthur's bed, and shook him.

'Uuugh! Wuss! Wuss!' went Arthur.

Ginny shook him harder. Arthur shot up in bed, saw Ginny, realised where he was, and frowned through bleary eyes.

'What the hell are you up to, Guinevere?' he said and scowled.

'I think I can hear voices outside, Arthur,' explained Ginny.

Arthur looked at his watch. He turned over.

'Ring the Police,' he mumbled.

'I think that someone may've kidnapped Len and Molly,' Ginny said urgently.

Arthur turned back to Ginny.

'Whaaaat?' he said.

'They're not in their room!' Ginny exclaimed.

Arthur came to his senses. Now, he certainly could hear voices. Something should be done, he decided. To Ginny's relief he swung his feet over the edge of the bed, and put on slippers and a dressing-gown. The children looked into Len and Molly's room. The Dickinsons were definitely not there. The children went downstairs and out of the open front door.

Outside, the weather was still, clear, and cold. The children shivered. A nearly full moon was visible high in the sky. There was a flickering light and voices were coming from an outhouse attached to the farm. The children crept over to the outhouse and noiselessly tried the door. It was locked. They saw that there was a short flight of stone steps on the outside of the outhouse. They climbed the steps, and the door at the top of the steps opened to their touch. Inside, they found a half landing with bales of hay and stairs up to it. The children peered over the bales of hay. They could not believe their eyes.

There were candles guttering in niches in the wall. Hanging in the centre was a hammer-like object. Two cowled figures were holding out their hands and bowing towards the hammer. With their forefingers, they were tracing out the shape of the hammer. The light flickered and the figures threw long shadows. The taller figure was intoning in a Yorkshire accent.

'. . . save us from the likes of Albert Lockey. Oh! Thor! Son of Odin! Protector of the Farmer! Wielder of the Hammer! Master of the Storm! Accept this offering of our devotion.'

The figure took out the strange knife that Arthur had found before and bent down over a frightened hen. He held the knife against the hen's neck. There was a small bowl underneath the hen to receive the offering of blood. Arthur was craning his neck. As he leaned forward, a pitchfork on top of the bales clattered on to the floor below. The figure whirled around, dropping the knife and the hen. The cowl dropped from his face. It was Leonard.

'Oy! You! Young scallywags from t' town, I'll be bound!' shouted Leonard. He raced up the stairs. Ginny was out in a shot. Arthur hesitated, and Leonard gave him a rugby tackle, bringing him to the floor. Leonard caught sight of Arthur's face.

'Arthur!' exclaimed Leonard. 'Well, I'll be blowed!'

Leonard was dumbfounded. Leonard and Arthur lay there, panting. The other cowled figure threw off its hood. It was Molly. She came up the steps and said,

'Arthur! What are you doin' here?'

Arthur sat up on the wooden floorboards of the half landing, his hair awry.

'We heard some noise and came to investigate,' he said, still gasping. 'We thought it might be burglars.'

Ginny was just outside and heard what had happened. She came back up the steps and on to the landing.

'Ah! There you are, Ginny! Get back to bed, both of you!' commanded Molly.

'Not until you tell us what you've been doing,' said Ginny.

Leonard stared at Ginny from the floor.

'It's none of your business!' he exclaimed.

'If anything's going on at this farm, I think we've got a right to know. Tell us what's happening!' demanded Ginny.

Leonard sat up on the floorboards and put his arms around his knees. He flexed his bony fingers. His eyes shifted from side to side, and he looked embarrassed.

'What do you think, Moother?' he asked, turning towards Molly.

Molly smoothed down her cloak, looking at the floor, and then rocked back on her heels, considering what to do.

'Well, Father,' she hesitantly concluded, 'now t' bairns have found us 'ere, I suppose we'll 'ave to tell 'em.'

Molly surveyed the scene.

'Look at you!' she exclaimed to the children. 'Get up off that floor, Arthur. You'll catch your death o' cold out 'ere. Let's go back in t' farm.'

Leonard and Arthur stood up slowly. They all trooped back into the farmhouse. The hen ran off, clucking.

'Mash us soom tea, Moother?' asked Leonard.

Leonard, Arthur, and Ginny sat in the living room in silence, while Molly brewed up some tea. The clock in the corner ticked loudly. Molly came into the living room with the tea, and Leonard began talking.

'Y'see, Arthur and Ginny, the rhymes are not the only tradition in our family,' he said. 'There's summat bin going on almost as far back as the original Leonard Dickinson.'

Leonard was nervously fingering an amulet around his neck. He looked strange, sitting there in his black cloak.

'Oh, I can't say!' he blurted, looking at Molly. 'You tell 'em, Moother!'

Molly took up the tale.

'It's the old gods, Arthur and Ginny,' she said. 'People way back used to worship them. But t' first Leonard Dickinson forbade 'is son from ivver doin' that. Then there came a time when it looked like there were goin' to be a bad harvest. The son took to prayin' to the gods. 'E found that Thor answered 'is prayers. And, that's what we still do in this family to this day. You may think it very strange an' foolish, boot we're joost simple coountry foolk and that's what we do.'

Molly stared down into her tea.

'You mean the Thor mentioned in the family rhyme? The Viking god Thor?' asked Ginny who had read about these things at school.

Leonard took the lead.

'Aye, it gooes back to those times, Ginny,' said Leonard. 'Y'see, Thor is t' protector of farmers and country folk. He is t' power be'ind t' rain and t' thunderstorm. We reckon as 'ow that thunderstorm last neet were an omen.'

'An omen of what?' queried Ginny. 'I heard you say something about an 'Albert Lockey'.'

'Do you want me to tell 'er, Moother?' asked Leonard, looking at Molly.

Molly nodded. She sipped at her tea.

'Albert Lockey is the town mayor,' continued Leonard. 'Since t' petrol rationin' started, t' town 'as been doin' little trade. That is, apart from Saturdays and Sundays. Now, Albert Lockey 'as got the traders behind 'im, and 'e intends to commercialise t' Moor. 'E 'opes to make Ilkley a major tourist attraction. Draw in t' crowds from Leeds and Bratford. It's queer 'ow yon Albert Lockey allus gets 'is own way. There's summat unnatural about 'im, from the tales folks are tellin'.'

Leonard stared thoughtfully into space, clasping his hands, and then remembered something.

"Ere, I've got a newspaper article.'

He pulled a local newspaper off the top of the radio and tossed it to the children. On the front page was an article entitled 'Ambitious plan to take Ilkley into 21st century'. The children read the article and saw that, apart from other things, Albert Lockey intended to have a full-scale model of the giant built at the Cow and Calf. In its head, it would have a revolving restaurant, lit at night. Also, he intended to have huge statues of Heathcliffe and Kathy, from the story *Wuthering Heights*, put up on the Moor and have a giant water slide at White Wells.

'They can't do that to my Moor,' said Ginny, possessively.

'Exactly', said Leonard, 'so that's why we were callin' on Thor for 'elp.'

There was a silence in which the clock in the corner chimed twice. Molly stood up, brushing down her cloak with her hands.

'Look at the time! It's two o'clock in t' morning. I think we've 'ad enough excitement for one neet,' she said. 'Off to bed, you two!'

'And mind you don't say nowt to nobody about this,' said Leonard, as the children went upstairs. The children took a long time to get to sleep and slept fitfully.

Len and Molly's Hammer

CHAPTER FOUR

A Rainy Saturday

The skies opened up, and rain poured forth. On the Moor, the Cow and Calf was enshrouded in mist. Dried-up streams had become raging torrents. In the town, there was a sheen on the slate roofs, reflecting the grey sky. The sky slipped into the gutters.

Because of what had happened the night before, Arthur and Ginny woke late.

When they had washed, dressed, and got downstairs, the Dickinsons were not around. Molly had left a note explaining that they had gone to market at Skipton. They always went on Saturdays and had decided to let the children lie in. The note told them to make their own breakfast and where to find things to make sandwiches for lunch, if they needed them. Molly had also left some money. No mention was made of the previous night, and the children decided not to say anything about it. They still could not believe what had happened.

The children rummaged in the cupboards in the kitchen, afraid to disturb anything of Molly's. They made themselves breakfast and managed to burn the toast. The rain was just as hard as when they had woken up. Arthur and Ginny discussed what they should do and decided to stay in. Their bikes were not due to arrive until Monday.

The morning dragged on, punctuated by the chiming of the clock. At first they amused themselves looking at everything in the living room. But they soon tired of that. They had not brought their personal stereos, so they could not even listen to any music. Eventually, Ginny was playing endless games of patience, while Arthur was fiddling with the radio. The loudspeaker was screeching, whining, and crackling. The air was filled with the throb of static. All at once, Ginny threw her cards down.

'Stop playing with that blinking thing!' shouted Ginny, above the noise of the radio. 'I'm bored.'

Arthur went over to her, grasped her hand, and shook it.

'How do you do? I'm Arthur,' he teased.

'Oh, very funny. Can't we go down into town? I don't think it's raining so hard, now,' Ginny pleaded.

Arthur switched off the radio. The children looked out of the window. The rain was not lashing the glass, as it had been five minutes ago. They decided to go out.

They made sandwiches, put on their waterproofs, left a note for Molly, and started down into town. Halfway into town, they realised that they had forgotten the flask.

The town had come alive. Along the Grove, there were hikers in multicoloured cagoules and anoraks. Many of the shops had opened up. The children walked along the Grove. There were several bookshops and many other types of shop. They bought postcards, envelopes, and writing paper at a newsagent's. They continued along the Grove. They admired the steeple of Christ Church on the right. Arthur spotted the date 1877 high up at the top of one building. They turned left at the end of the Grove into Brook Street.

In Brook Street, the children could see no brook. The street seemed to be full of bakers, building societies, and banks. The street led down to All Saints Church at some traffic lights. The children bought some cans of fizzy drink at another newsagent's. Arthur stared fascinated at the televisions in an electrical shop. Then he jumped at the scene on the screens. There was a man, looking tired and unshaven and sitting hunched up at a table. His eyes looked bruised, as if he had been beaten up. Arthur thought the man looked a bit like his father.

'Ginny!' Arthur called. 'Quick! Look at this!'

Ginny came dashing over and was only just in time to catch a glimpse of the man before the image vanished from the screens.

'Our Dad!' Ginny wailed. 'I think he's been captured by Sheikh Ranish in the Middle East.'

The children pushed their way into the newsagent's and bought a paper, but the headline was about the latest scandal involving a cabinet minister. His mistress appeared nude in the centre pages.

Ginny was on the verge of tears. Arthur grabbed her by the shoulders.

'Now, look, Gin,' he said, 'we're not really sure it's Dad. There's nothing we can do, and I'm sure you don't want Mum worrying about us. Promise you'll not make a fuss.'

'Yes . . .' sobbed Ginny, wiping her eyes. The rain was mixing with her tears.

'Calm down!' instructed Arthur. 'Let's visit the manor house.'

They set off down Brook Street, and when they reached Church Street, the children saw that they had missed the various signs clearly pointing to The Manor House. Ginny had stopped crying. She had decided not to mention her worries about her Dad to Arthur for the rest of the day. As they sheltered in the passageway leading to the cobbled courtyard, they saw that the entrance to the manor house was open and dashed through it. They took off and shook out their outer clothing. Ginny was beginning to feel a little better and forget her troubles. Arthur was concerned about the situation but showed nothing outwardly. They started to look around.

Through a door to the right, was a stone-flagged room with a large fireplace in it. A clock in the room had struck twelve as the children walked in. Ginny noticed that the clock displayed the phases of the moon. The mantelshelf of the fire had various old pieces of earthenware and pewter on top of it. In the fireplace were hanging some copper pots and pans. Arthur stood in the fireplace and looked up the chimney. He could just see some light. In the room, there were ancient pieces of furniture including an old sette and some old chests. One of the chests was adapted to take money. The children put some through the slot. There were also paintings of Wharfedale in times gone by.

Tiring of this, the children made their way through into the next room. It contained a display of the history of Ilkley. They looked at a printed explanation of the reasons why a Roman Fort had been built at this place. To one side, they saw two Roman gravestones. One carving was of a family but there was no inscription. The other was more interesting. There was a carving of a woman wearing a flowing tunic and with plaits in her hair. Underneath was an inscription, from which they gathered that the woman's name was Velnica. She had died when she was only thirty years old.

Moving on from the gravestones, the children noticed some photographs on the wall. They were of the rocks marked 'cup and ring'. They saw one of the Swastika Stone. A sign described the markings and said,

. . . Many theories have been advanced as to their meaning—astrological, magical, genealogical, tribal, and so on—but their significance remains an enigma.

The children browsed a bit longer. Arthur was amused by a blown-up advert for The Ilkley Couch, which said that it was 'far ahead of any other Appliance for the relief of SUFFERING HUMANITY'. The couch had been used when Ilkley was a spa town and people came here to take the waters. They used to believe that the water would cure all sorts of ailments. The children finally went upstairs to a exhibition of paintings by a modern painter. They did not like the paintings.

All this time, the children had been drinking from the cans that they had bought. They were just going back out of the entrance door, when a woman, who had been sitting reading a book in a side-office, called out,

'You shouldn't really drink in here!'

'We're just going out,' said Ginny.

'OK, then', said the woman, 'are those cans finished?'

Arthur and Ginny nodded.

'Then don't throw them away. Give them to me,' said the woman. 'I'll take them to the can bank. Green by name and green by nature.'

The woman came over, took the cans, and introduced herself as Alison Green. She was in her late twenties, had fair hair, and was wearing spectacles, a T-shirt, a long black skirt, and trainers. She discovered that the children were staying at Folfoot Farm with their grandparents.

'And you know why it's called Folfoot Farm?' asked Alison.

The children said that they did not know why.

'The Swastika, Celtic Rose, Gammadion, or Fylfot. Folfoot is a corruption of Fylfot,' Alison explained knowledgeably.

'You mean, because of the Swastika Stone, just above the farm?' queried Ginny.

'That's right,' said Alison. 'Of course, there is another name for the Swastika. The Hammer of Thor.'

The children stood there, aghast.

'. . . The Hammer it is lost to Thor . . .' recited Arthur.

'What's that?' asked Alison.

'Oh, nothing,' said Arthur innocently.

Alison asked the children if they were interested in the Roman Fort. They said, 'Yes.' The rain was holding off for a bit, so she took them around the corner of the manor house. There she showed them the excavated remains of the west wall of the fort. Arthur was still interested in the stones on the Moor.

'I was wondering, just how many cup-and-ring-marked rocks are there on the Moor?' asked Arthur.

'At the last count, we know of at least two hundred of them,' said Alison.

'Perhaps you can show me a few on my map,' enquired Arthur.

Alison studied her watch.

'It's about one, and I've got to close up the manor house,' said Alison. 'But, I'll tell you what, tomorrow is Sunday, and it's my day off. What would you say if we went up on the Moor, and I showed you some of the markings?'

The children were delighted. Alison told them to ask their grandparents first. She said that they would know her. They agreed to meet by the Cow and Calf kiosk at nine thirty the following day. Alison showed the children where the kiosk was on the map.

It started raining more heavily. The children were forced to put on their waterproofs again. Alison dashed back into the manor house. The children went up the steps to All Saints Church. As they went past the tower of the church, the clock struck one. They studied the face of the clock for a moment. They then went into the porch of the church, sat down on some stone seats, and decided to eat their sandwiches there. They were a bit worried that someone might stop them, but no one did.

After they had finished their sandwiches, Arthur decided that he wanted to investigate some things in the local library. He found it next to the town hall on the town plan, and the children were soon standing outside the library.

There were reliefs of faces and figures in the front face of the building. The children did not know of whom. The clock on the town hall was pointing to one thirty. On entering the library, the children saw that it closed at two on a Saturday. An infrared beam was interrupted on entering, and a counter clicked. The children took off their wet-weather gear and stowed it in their rucksack. Arthur enquired about the legend of the giant at the main counter, and they were given a set of keys for the bookcases in the Local History section. They entered a side-room with glass-fronted cases of books against the wall. They opened one of the cases and started browsing.

There were books on every imaginable topic concerning Ilkley and Yorkshire. The botany, archaeology, and geology of Wharfedale were all described. Ginny found a book on Practical Hydropathy, with diagrams of internal organs in it. She guessed that Hydropathy was the science of the water cure that had been practised at Ilkley.

Arthur was reaching for a large, old book with the title *Pedigrees of the County Families of Yorkshire*, when it flopped on to the floor. A yellowing parchment fell out, upside down. He picked it up, turned it over, and read,

Two and Two are Foure,
Foure and Foure are Ayte,
Look thou at my Feete,
And find ye Ring of Fayte.

Twelve sat downe,
At ye Last Feaste,
Look thou Inside me,
And find ye Cuppe of Peace.

Maiden, wear ye Ring,
Maiden, drink Wyne from ye Cuppe,
Stand thou on ye Badger,
When ye Full moon is juste uppe.

Stand thou on ye Rock,
At ye Sun Ryse,
Then he who holds ye Hammer,
Shall have Power and be Wyse.

At the bottom of the parchment were also the initials, LD, and the date, 1670.

Arthur gave a low whistle and turned to Ginny.

'Look at this, Ginny,' he said excitedly.

Ginny read the parchment and said, 'Here's a real mystery, Arthur. Could the initials, LD, be Leonard Dickinson?'

'You bet!' said Arthur. 'He's telling us where the cup and ring are.'

'I think we'd better photocopy this and put it back,' said Ginny.

They put some money in the photocopier; it whirred and made a copy, which Arthur put in his rucksack. The town-hall clock had already struck two. The children were intent on studying the parchment, wondering what it could mean. Just then a handsome middle-aged man with bright red hair breezed in, saw the children, and went over to them.

'Come on now, the library is closing,' the man said. 'I can't have scruffy-looking children hanging around. Who are you anyway? I don't seem to recognise you.'

'We are not scruffy-looking children,' returned Arthur. 'And I might as well ask you who you are.'

'Albert Lockey,' snapped the man. 'And who are you, may I ask?'

'James and Jenny,' said Arthur, giving Albert Lockey the first names that came into his head.

Albert Lockey looked at them and then saw the parchment.

'What's this?' he said. 'Trying to steal council property? I'll have that!'

He snatched the parchment off them and then said, 'I'm not having young brats coming into my library and stealing things. Off with you!'

With that, Albert Lockey grabbed the children by the shoulders and wheeled them, protesting, out of the library. Arthur just succeeded in getting hold of his rucksack and taking it out with him.

Outside, it had stopped raining. The children walked along the street, quite annoyed, and sat down at a waterless fountain at the head of Brook Street.

'Of all the cheek!' exclaimed Ginny. 'That's the town mayor Len and Molly told us about. What a nasty piece of work!'

'Well, anyway, we have a copy of the parchment,' said Arthur. 'I only hope Albert Lockey doesn't manage to work out what it's all about.'

'Why don't we tell Len and Molly?' queried Ginny.

'Look, Ginny,' said Arthur. 'I've been thinking about that. It's our secret. If we can figure out the rhymes, it'll be much more fun that way.'

After having another look at the copy of the parchment, the children started on the way home. Ginny sensed that Arthur was up to something. On the Grove, he bought a map of the whole of Wharfedale.

When the children got back to Folfoot Farm, Len and Molly had returned.

'It were fair silin' it down today, weren't it?' said Molly. 'What 'ave you been oop to?'

The children told Molly where they had been, but left out any reference to the parchment that they had found or to Albert Lockey. They mentioned their meeting with Alison Green, and Molly said that it was all right to go on the Moor with her. Molly also said that Alison knew a lot about Ilkley and the Moor. Ginny suddenly remembered seeing the man on the television.

'Molly!' she cried. 'We think Sheikh Ranish has got Dad.'

'Why ivver do you think that?' Molly asked.

'We saw a captured man on a television in Brook Street!' Ginny exclaimed.

'You moost've imagined it,' said Molly. 'That could nivver 'appen to David. 'E's too clever.'

The children were beginning to believe that they had been mistaken. They made no further mention of their worries.

Later that evening, when they had finished their tea and were sitting down together, Arthur was trying to find out something.

'Len,' he said, 'would you know anyone who would be able to figure out the directions of sunrises and sunsets?'

'That's a strange request,' Leonard said. 'Boot there is someone in Ilkley. Everyone knows 'im as The Captain. Me and 'im were doin' National service together in t' Royal Navy. Used to teach navigation. 'E would know. Why don't you ring 'im up? I'll find t' number.'

Arthur got on the phone. When he had dialled the number, a cheerful voice answered. He enquired who it was and gathered that it was The Captain. He explained who he was and what he wanted.

'I don't know,' The Captain replied. 'I haven't done spherical trig for twenty-five years. I think I've still got my Norie's tables. I may need a nautical almanac. I'll see what I can do, and I'll send you a letter. What's your address?'

Arthur told The Captain where he was staying and thanked him for his help, before he hung up.

That night, Ginny was so exhausted that she slept easily, but Arthur was up till all hours, looking at the copy of the parchment and studying his maps of Ilkley Moor.

CHAPTER FIVE

The Cow and Calf

Curlews were calling from the Moor. The children peeked around the edge of the curtain in their room and looked out. The sun was touching the tops of the trees and little, fluffy clouds were drifting lazily past. It looked like it was going to be a fine day.

This morning, Ginny had set her alarm. When she woke, Arthur was still asleep. She woke him as they had to be on their way early.

Their breakfast was not as big this day as it had been the day before. Molly was getting used to their wishes. Leonard came in with the Sunday papers.

'Bad news', he said, 'it seems you were right about your father.'

He showed the children a headline. It read,

'British airmen held by Ranish'

The children read the article. It said that Sheikh Ranish was holding their father until the United Nations made certain concessions over the war.

Ginny's lower lip was trembling, and her eyes were wet.

'Now, then, lass,' said Leonard, patting Ginny's shoulder, 'I'm sure that our Government is doin' awl it can. Remember, you're goin' oop to t' Cow an' Calf today, and you've got awl t' Moor to explore. Dry your eyes. Here . . .'

He handed Ginny his handkerchief. Ginny wiped her eyes and gradually pulled herself together. Leonard went out into the farmyard.

'Let's be off, Arthur!' she finally exclaimed, giving him a weak smile.

When Arthur and Ginny were putting on their walking boots, Molly had some instructions for them.

'Mind you, be'ave thisen whilst your on t' Moor with Alison Green,' she told them. 'We don't want 'er sayin' that we don't know 'ow to look after children.'

This time, the children made sure that they took a flask, some dried milk, and some tea bags with them. Molly had already made some sandwiches. Arthur packed them in his rucksack. When the children got outside, Jess came bounding up to meet them, barking. They patted her and stroked her head.

Leonard, who had started work in the stable and was mucking out Bracken, called them over.

'Ave a good day on t' Moor, children,' he said, winking at Ginny.

The children said that they would. Leonard took a long look at Arthur.

'Arthur,' he said, sternly, 'I reckon as 'ow you're oop to summat. Don't go meddlin' with things that don't concern you. Think on.'

Arthur just put on his innocent look, and the children set off.

They knew the way into the town well enough by now. It was busy with cyclists and walkers. In the town, they went along the Grove, past the library, and, following a sign that said Cow and Calf Rocks, they started up a steep climb on the other side.

Eventually, just after a beck running down the hillside, they went over a cattle grid. There were larger crags above the children here. On the end of the crags was a stone that looked exactly like a crocodile's open mouth. Continuing the climb, Arthur began singing at the top of his voice,

Wheer wor ta bahn when ah saw thee,
Ooon Iiilkla Moooor baaaht 'aaaat?

'Very good, Arthur,' said Ginny. 'You should be on the stage.'

'What, the first stage out of town, Ginny?' sniggered Arthur.

'Don't you ever give up, Arthur?' rejoined Ginny. 'I've got a joke for you. What's the difference between ignorance and apathy?'

'Go on!' beamed Arthur. 'What's the difference between ignorance and apathy?'

'I don't know, and I don't care!' Ginny cried out, holding her arms wide and swinging around.

Both children laughed. Arthur was glad that Ginny was still able to tell jokes, despite not knowing what would happen to their father.

The children continued on up the hill, taking in draughts of the pure, cold air. The Cow Rock loomed over them. Ginny suddenly stopped and pointed.

'Look at that, Arthur!' she cried.

Painted on the Cow Rock in large white letters they saw the words,

STOP DEVELOPMENT ON THE MOOR

'At least someone's bothered by what Albert Lockey's trying to do,' Ginny commented. 'But did they really need to do that?'

The Cow and Calf Rocks

The Cottage or Haystack Stone

They arrived at the Cow and Calf car park and found the kiosk on the dot of nine thirty. The kiosk was not yet open, but it would be later. It served food and drink to the walkers and cyclists but only on Saturdays and Sundays when there were enough people. Alison Green was not there.

Then the children heard a car approaching. A Range Rover wheeled into the car park with its horn sounding. Alison Green was in the car. She drew to a halt, turned off the engine, and got out. She was wearing a green nylon anorak and walking trousers. She spotted the children.

'Hello, Ginny and Arthur!' she called.

The children went over to the Range Rover.

'Where did you get the fuel for that?' asked Ginny. 'Doesn't it use rather a lot of petrol?'

Alison looked annoyed. 'Where I got the fuel is none of your business!' she snapped. 'And what car I drive is entirely up to me!' She rummaged angrily in the back of the car and found and put on a pair of boots. She turned around, gazed at the Cow and Calf, and then brightened visibly.

'Ah! It's good to be back on the Moor!' she exclaimed, taking in deep breaths of the air and then turned to the children. 'You're all set?' she enquired.

The children nodded.

'Then first I'll show you the Cow and Calf Quarry.'

They went up the hillside to the left of the Cow and Calf rocks. Alison took them into the quarry. It had been disused for many years. Alison explained that the millstone grit had been used for building material. She said that the millstone grit was formed in the Carboniferous period, over 325 million years ago, in the delta of a river that had been here. She pointed out some bands in the rock, which she said were an example of cross bedding. They went around the corner and climbed up to the ridge by the side of the Cow Rock. They got on to the Cow Rock by using a couple of very worn footholds. From the top, they could see the whole of Ilkley spread out before them. They could see down on to the Calf Rock. It was very windy and exposed here. Alison asked the children if they been told the legend of Giant Rombald.

'Oh, yes, Alison,' said Ginny, 'our grandad told us.'

'Well, if you look over there, you'll see Almscliff Crag,' said Alison, pointing.

The children saw the silhouette on the horizon that they had seen before from the Swastika Stone. Now it was much nearer.

'There is another legend . . . ,' continued Alison.

The children pricked up their ears.

'Except, it's true,' said Alison. 'There once was a hermit on Ilkley Moor. His name was Job Senior. He liked his drink, and people used to come to hear him sing. It is said by some people that he had a rather fine voice, but others say that they paid him to stop singing. There's now a pub near Burley Woodhead, called the Hermit.'

The Sunday bells of All Saints Church had started ringing. Alison pointed down the Wharfe valley at the river way below them.

'You see that bend in the river down there at manor park?' she enquired.

The children nodded.

'That's where the glacier that was once in this valley left a terminal moraine,' Alison explained. 'It dammed up the river and a lake formed. You can see the playing fields on the flat land where the bed of the lake was. The river broke through the moraine, and that's why it suddenly bends there.'

The children continued looking around. The top of the Cow Rock was covered with markings where people had carved their names. Ginny and Arthur could not believe some of the dates carved. Alison pointed out the Giant's Footprint, and some religious inscriptions. The children could make out.

... LORD JESUS CHRIST AND THOU SHALT ...

Next, Alison took the children south along the ridge to a small boulder standing on it. The children saw a plaque set into the boulder. It read,

SING TO GOD,
SING PRAISES TO HIS NAME,
LIFT UP A SONG TO HIM,
WHO RIDES UPON THE CLOUDS;

HIS NAME IS THE LORD,
EXULT BEFORE HIM.
PSALM 68/4.

'They say that that inscription is there so that people will read it and change their minds before they throw themselves off the Cow Rock,' said Alison.

The children shivered. 'What an awful way to die,' they thought.

They were walking near the top of the quarry. Sheep were scattering away from them. Alison told them that the sheep were of a breed known as Swaledale. As they were continuing to the next ridge above the Cow and Calf, Alison bent down and pointed out two plants growing almost side by side.

'That's bilberry and that's crowberry,' she said. 'The crowberry is taking over from the heather on the Moor. Try one.'

She picked a small, black crowberry and gave it to Ginny. Ginny popped it in her mouth. She bit on the berry and tasted it.

'Mmmm,' she said. 'It doesn't taste of anything.'

Alison smiled. 'The bilberries taste much nicer, however,' she commented. 'But you need quite a few before you've got enough for a pie!'

Ginny spat out the berry. They were walking up a track carved into the ridge. Alison stopped to talk to the children.

'These tracks on to the Moor are thought either to have been made by peat cutters or by miners,' she said.

'There has been some mining activity on the Moor, particularly at Lanshaw Delves,' she continued. 'That place is a lateral moraine, left over from when Wharfedale was glaciated in the Ice Age, about eleven thousand years ago.'

'Like the moraine at manor park?' asked Ginny.

Alison confirmed that both moraines were left by the same glacier. They continued to the top of the ridge, where Alison stopped again.

'You know that the scenery here is man-made,' she said to the children. 'By examining pollen buried in the peat, we can tell that there was originally woodland here. It seems that early man gradually cut it all down.'

'So why doesn't it grow again?' enquired Arthur.

'That's easy,' answered Alison. 'The sheep eat any trees that start to grow up here.'

There was a large boulder nearby. Alison led Arthur and Ginny over to it.

'This is the Haystack Stone,' said Alison, patting the rock. 'There are cup and ring marks on the top of this.'

Arthur was able to get on top of the stone. It only stood about head high. Sure enough, Arthur could make out markings on it.

'You probably know', explained Alison, 'that nobody is really sure what these markings mean. As far as we can tell, most of them date from the Late Neolithic. However, we can't tell if the markings were carved all in one go or over a period of time. All that can be seen is the remnants of the carvings. They could even have been painted, in the same way that Aborigines colour stones in Australia. Now, they are gradually being eroded by the effects of acid rain.'

Arthur jumped down from the rock.

'There is one rock I know that is absolutely covered in these marks,' continued Alison.

'What rock is that, Alison?' asked Arthur, his ears pricking up again.

'The Badger Stone,' said Alison.

'Stand thou on the Badger, when the Full Moon is just up . . . ,' recited Arthur, in a low voice.

'You mumble to yourself sometimes, you know, Arthur,' commented Alison.

Arthur ignored the remark. 'Where is the Badger Stone?' he asked.

'Just above Barmishaw Wood, beyond White Wells,' said Alison. 'I'll take you there, if you like.'

Arthur looked agitated.

'Thank you very much, but we'd better be off, now,' he said quickly.

'What, already?' said Alison, surprised. 'I was going to show you the Backstone Beck enclosure and then take you through Rocky Valley. There is a stone with some fossils in it there.'

'Thanks very much for showing us around, Alison,' said Arthur, grabbing Ginny's hand, 'but I think we'd better be going.'

'Very well, then,' conceded Alison. 'Are you sure you'll be all right by yourselves?'

Arthur assured Alison that they could look after themselves and immediately started leading Ginny towards a beck that flowed down the moorside. Alison strode off towards the Cow and Calf.

'What was that all about, Arthur?' queried Ginny.

'I am beginning to get the feeling that we are bound up in something big,' said Arthur earnestly. 'It's all coming together, and I don't think we have much time to solve the riddles. I thought perhaps if we went up on the Moor and had a look at a few things, we would solve them.'

Arthur led Ginny up the moorside towards the beck. A startled flock of grouse burst up from under their feet, their wings clattering, and flew up into the air. 'Go back! Go back! Go back!' they called. The sun was going in. The children went down to the beck and started to cross it. All at once, Arthur slipped on a greasy stone in the beck, fell awkwardly against the bank, and they heard the flask in his rucksack shatter.

Arthur got the flask out of his rucksack and shook it. It made a sloshing sound from the many slivers of glass inside, but it was not leaking. He put it back in his pack.

'No more tea, Ilkley Moor or otherwise,' he commented.

The sky was darkening. They rounded a corner in the beck. There was a dead sheep in the stream. Its glazed eyes stared heavenwards, and flies buzzed around it. There was a smell of putrescence in the air. Suddenly, an evil-looking magpie flew down and started ripping at the rotting flesh.

'I don't like it!' wailed Ginny.

At that moment, there was a shouting and screaming noise from behind them. They whirled around. Someone was charging through the bracken. The children wanted to run away, but they were rooted to the spot by terror. Suddenly, a wild-eyed, unkempt man burst out of the bracken and grabbed both of the children by the scruff of their necks.

'You're from the Police, aren't you?' he screamed, shaking them. 'Eyes! Eyes! Looking at me!'

'We're not from the Police!' shouted Arthur. 'We've got nothing to do with them!'

The man suddenly dropped the children and crouched down on his haunches, weeping. 'Oh, I'm sorry. I'm so sorry,' he sobbed.

Now the man did not look like the monster he had seemed a few moments ago. He looked quite pitiful. He was unshaven and was wearing a soft leather cowboy jacket with tassels on it. His shirt and jeans were creased and dirty. Ginny guessed that he was about thirty-five years old. Ginny was holding back, but Arthur took the lead.

'What's your name?' he asked.

'Jim,' said the man.

'And where have you come from, Jim?' Arthur continued.

'I used to be in a mental hospital, but they closed it down,' said Jim. 'Now I live on the Moor over there. I've got nowhere else to go.'

Jim pointed out a small ruined building. Only the walls remained. Arthur and Ginny could see some black plastic sheeting over it. Ginny touched Arthur on the shoulder and drew him aside.

'Are you sure we should have anything to do with this strange man?' she whispered to Arthur. 'You know what we've always been taught.'

'You keep quiet, Ginny!' said Arthur. 'I know what I'm doing.'

Arthur led Ginny and Jim over to the ruin. The children discovered, from the few words Jim said, that there was a mental hospital near the Moor. Jim lay down on a bed of bracken and heather inside his camp. Arthur saw an old Primus stove. Under Jim's directions, he got it going, got some water from the beck in a pan, and found some cracked, dirty cups. He used his own tea bags and dried milk, and they were soon sitting crouched down and drinking tea. It was peaty and had bits floating in it, but it was tea. Arthur offered Jim a sandwich, but he refused.

The sun had come out again.

'You know, Jim, I was once in a mental hospital,' Arthur said. 'I got hit on the head while out playing, walked off, and was found by the Police wandering around a derelict house. I didn't know who I was, and I had to go into hospital for a while. I imagined someone was going to kill me.'

Arthur looked down at the ground.

'I still feel funny sometimes,' he said sadly.

Jim nodded. He understood. Ginny was looking worried. She was still afraid of Jim.

'Don't worry, Gin!' soothed Arthur, patting Ginny's knee. 'It's not as bad as you think.'

'You know what, Jim, you're the Hermit of Ilkley Moor!' Arthur laughed.

It broke the tension. They all laughed. Soon they were chatting. After a while, Arthur started reaching into his rucksack. He drew out the copy of the parchment. He began to show it to Jim.

'I thought you said that was our secret, Arthur,' commented Ginny when she saw.

'Jim might be able to work out these nutty rhymes,' said Arthur. 'Besides, who is Jim going to tell up here?'

Arthur read out the first verse on the copy.

> Two and Two are Four,
> Four and Four are Eight,
> Look thou at my Feet,
> And find ye Ring of Fate.

'Do you know what that means, Jim?' he asked.

Jim's eyes took on a wild look again. He started shaking slightly.

'Doubling, doubling, always doubling,' he said in a high, cracked voice. 'Double, double, toil and trouble. Double my troubles. Doubler. Doubler.'

Arthur got out his map and studied it.

'That's it!' he cried. 'The Doubler Stones! They're here on the map!'

Arthur showed the map to Ginny and then he read out the verse again.

> Two and Two are Four,
> Four and Four are Eight,
> Look thou at my Feet,
> And find ye Ring of Fate.

'We've got to go to the Doubler Stones and find a ring, somewhere at the foot of them,' he said excitedly.

The children could not wait to get away. They made their excuses and carried on up the beck, from where a path led down to Rocky Valley. The last they saw of Jim that day, he was sitting on the ground, his arms around his knees, rocking backwards and forward, and singing softly to himself.

CHAPTER SIX

The Badger Stone

The clouds were increasing. Patches of sunlight and darkness rolled across the Moor, and the wind was getting up.

The children were making their way towards Rocky Valley, debating with each other as to what they should do next.

'Let's go to the Doubler Stones now!' exclaimed Ginny, excitedly.

'I've looked at the map, and it's too far,' explained Arthur.

'Since you say we've not got much time, why can't we go?' said Ginny impatiently.

'I won't know how much time we've got, until I receive the letter I'm expecting from The Captain, will I?' snapped Arthur.

'Why don't we go anyway, Arthur?' repeated Ginny.

'Our bikes arrive on Monday. That's tomorrow. We can go then. That's final,' concluded Arthur.

The children continued across the Moor, both a little bit miffed with each other, but soon forgot about it on reaching Rocky Valley. A panorama of the whole of Ilkley was spread before them.

'It's lovely, isn't it, Arthur?' enthused Ginny.

Arthur was lost in his own thoughts. 'Let's go to the Badger Stone,' he said.

'Why's that?' demanded Ginny.

'We might as well find out where it is,' said Arthur. 'I think we're going to need to know that.'

The sun had gone in again. The children were at the western end of Rocky Valley. They went down some steps into the valley and started descending towards White Wells. The dead bracken was shifting restlessly in the breeze.

White Wells

The Plunge Bath at White Wells

The children reached White Wells in a blaze of sunshine. The children found a couple of connected cottages, painted brilliant white. There were signs of habitation, with net curtains in the windows and some washing hanging out. Arthur and Ginny went around to the front, where they saw a door with BATHS inscribed above it. Another door was open. Inside, they found a plunge bath, made of local stone, set into the floor. There were steps down to the bath and railings around it. The water running into it made a constant gurgling sound. There was a gargoyle through which the water poured, and small, green ferns were growing out of the walls of the bath. Many people had thrown money into the bath. Arthur and Ginny threw some money in and made wishes.

'Bet you're wishing for Dad,' said Arthur.

'It's a secret wish, Arthur,' said Ginny. 'I'm not supposed to tell you.'

The children looked around. To one side, there was a display of fossils found on the Moor, and, up some steps, there was a display giving the history of the water cure at Ilkley. The children discovered that Charles Darwin, who first proposed the theory of evolution, and possibly Delius, the composer, had come to White Wells. They purchased some tea and wholemeal fruitcake from the couple that lived there. They also bought some cartons of fruit juice. Arthur and Ginny got into conversation with the couple and discovered that the well was not Roman, but had been built in 1756 by the local landowner, Squire Middleton, for people taking the water cure. The couple also mentioned 'Donkey' Jackson, who used to hire out donkeys to the Victorians to bring them up to White Wells from the centre of Ilkley.

The children went outside with their tea and fruitcake and ate their sandwiches. They kept some of the sandwiches for later.

Just as they were enjoying the view, a van roared up the track to White Wells. Some men wearing safety helmets and fluorescent jackets got out of the van and proceeded to take out surveying instruments. They were wandering over the Moor nearby, taking measurements and notes. The children wondered what the men were up to, but they were aware that time was getting on and they had to be on their way.

The children packed up their things, took their cups and plates back to the couple, and set off again. Arthur was looking at the map. Under his direction, they started up the hillside behind White Wells and hit a well-trodden path. The sun had gone in completely. Soon, they reached a lonely wood of Scotch Pine. There was a large stone at the head of the wood. The children looked at it. It had cup and ring markings on it.

'Is this the Badger Stone, Arthur?' asked Ginny.

'No, it's further over, above the next wood, I think,' replied Arthur.

The wind was whistling through the wood. A magpie was hopping from branch to branch and cackling. They were glad to get away from this strange, desolate place.

The children tramped on in silence. They reached the next wood and climbed up a rock-strewn gully to one side. The only sound that could be heard was the wind hissing in the grass and the buzz of flies in the wood. On reaching the top, they hunted around a bit and eventually found a cup-and-ring-marked rock.

'Now, is this the Badger Stone, Arthur?' queried Ginny.

'I really don't know, Ginny,' answered Arthur. 'It seems right, from what Alison Green said.'

They sat down on the rock. They rested there dejectedly in the gloom. The midges were descending in droves to bite them. Just then, Ginny spotted a figure striding purposefully across the Moor from the west. As the figure got nearer, the children could make out a tall, muscular man with red hair and a beard. He was wearing a lumberjack shirt and had a safety helmet on his head.

'Could you tell me if this is the Badger Stone?' Ginny, when the man approached.

'Certainly. This is not the Badger Stone. This is the Barmishaw Stone,' replied the man, in a foreign-sounding accent. 'The Badger Stone is up yonder about a half a mile away.'

The man pointed south, up the rise of the Moor. The children thanked the man and were about to move on, when he said, 'I am a geologist, and I have lost my geological hammer somewhere near here. Have you seen it?'

The 'Willy Hall's Wood' Stone.

The Barmishaw Stone

The children said that they had not seen a hammer anywhere and continued on their way. They followed a path that looked almost like a sheep-track. When Ginny looked back, the geologist was nowhere to be seen. The Moor had swallowed him up as if he had never existed.

There was some watery sunshine now. Presently, the children spotted a wooden bench with a rock beside it, rising out of the Moor like a humpbacked whale. On looking at the far side of the rock, the children could see that it was covered with cup and ring marks. This was the Badger Stone.

The Badger Stone

It was a bit fresher up here, and there were not so many midges. The children sat down on the bench and ate the last of their sandwiches. They drank from their cartons. An inquisitive sheep came up in the hopes of getting some food. Arthur teased it by making baaing noises at it. Ginny shooed it away. Arthur was rummaging in his rucksack. He drew out two pieces of wire coat-hanger, bent at right angles, and two biro cases. He inserted the wire into the cases. He was making dowsing rods.

'Not those things,' commented Ginny, when she saw. 'You know what Great-Aunt Betty said.'

'I know what I'm doing,' said Arthur, crossly. 'There's no danger. You're too superstitious.'

Arthur started to pace around the Badger Stone, holding out the dowsing rods. He held the rods parallel to one another. He noted at what point he was on the ground when the rods turned in his hands and crossed over themselves. He noticed that as he moved away from the Stone, either northward or southward, the rods crossed and uncrossed about every five paces. Every time he crossed the east—west line of the ridge of the Stone, the rods also crossed.

Eventually, he came over to Ginny.

'I'm definitely getting a reaction along an east—west axis,' he said. 'I think there is some old association with sunrise and sunset.'

'You don't really believe those dowsing rods,' said Ginny, contemptuously. 'You get what you expect to get with them.'

There was a lady out walking two Irish setters, coming across the Moor. She was wearing a tweed skirt and a matching hat, and a waxed cotton jacket. She recognised the children and came over. It was Madeleine English from All Saints Church. She greeted the children and then caught sight of the dowsing rods.

'Are those dowsing rods?' she demanded.

'Yes,' answered Arthur. 'I'm just investigating the charged fields around the Badger Stone.'

'And are you getting any kind of reaction?' Madeleine queried.

'Yes,' replied Arthur. 'There's definitely something along an east—west axis.'

'I can't explain now', said Madeleine, looking worried, 'but you want to look out if you are getting vibes off old stones. Believe me.'

Arthur played the whole thing down, and Madeleine went off with her dogs. It was starting to rain. The children packed up their things and got into their waterproofs. They continued over the Moor, across a beck and the Keighley Road to the Swastika Stone, and, from there, back to Folfoot Farm.

When the children got back, Leonard was in the kitchen talking to Molly and looking very angry.

'What's the matter, Len?' asked Ginny.

'Look at this!' Leonard shouted, waving an official-looking document at Ginny.

The children looked at the document.

'It's Albert Lockey,' fumed Leonard. "E's put a compulsory purchase order on this farm. They're gonner knock it down and build the Folfoot Housing Estate 'ere.' Leonard looked red in the face and flapped his arms.

'And 'e's got the go-ahead to start work on t' Moor. It's a disgrace, but there's nowt we can do about it. The 'ole council are be'ind 'im.'

'We saw some men up at White Wells,' said Ginny.

'That'll be them,' barked Leonard. 'They start work in a week's time. I don't know what t' world's coming to.'

Leonard was out of sorts the whole evening. Molly clattered angrily in the kitchen. The children went to bed, determined to do something about the situation.

Ginny woke briefly during the night and heard voices from the outhouse. She went back to sleep. She knew what it was. Leonard and Molly had their son-in-law as well as Albert Lockey's plans to worry about now.

CHAPTER SEVEN

The Doubler Stones

Ginny looked out of the bedroom window. She could see Molly hanging out the washing. The washing was rising and falling on the line and billowing and flapping in the breeze.

'Monday is washing day!' thought Ginny.

The early-morning sun glinted in the pools of rain, left over from the night before.

When the children got down from their room, there were two letters for them. They recognised their mother's handwriting on the first one. They opened it and read the letter.

> *My dearest darlings,*
> *You have probably heard by now that David has been captured after being shot down. Don't worry, my darlings. I'm sure there is a way out of this. Meanwhile I want you to be as brave as your father is. He loves you, as I do, and I'm sure he wouldn't want you fretting about him. Be a credit to him in the days to follow.*
> *My prayers are with both you and David.*
> *God bless.*

It was signed by their mother with kisses underneath. Both the children held back their tears. They would obey their mother and be strong.

The other letter was for Arthur. He opened it and out fell three little pieces of paper. There was a main letter, which Arthur read over breakfast. The letter was from The Captain, and it had been desktop published on his home computer. When Arthur finished reading it, he told Ginny that they had better hold a council of war. After breakfast, they sat on their beds in their room and discussed the situation.

'The first thing is', said Arthur, 'that we were so pleased to have worked out the first verse on the parchment that we didn't ask Jim if he knew what the other verses meant.'

'We'll have to go back up to the Cow and Calf and find him,' said Ginny.

'Yes,' said Arthur. 'But there's something more important. I was interested in the line between the Cow and Calf and Almscliff Crag.'

'Why's that?' demanded Ginny.

'Haven't you ever read *The Old Straight Track* by Alfred Watkins?' returned Arthur. 'It's all about ancient lines of power called ley lines.'

'No, I haven't read that book. What's that got to do with us?' queried Ginny.

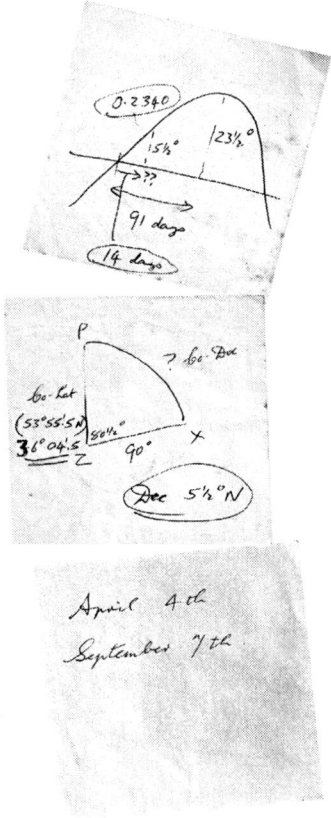

Three Little Pieces of Paper

'I'll explain,' continued Arthur. 'It's all to do with the legend of Giant Rombald. Legends sometimes have some truth in them. What the legend indicates is that there's something to do with the sunrise over Almscliff Crag, as viewed from the Cow and Calf. You know what The Captain says about that?'

'No. What?' asked Ginny, getting interested.

'He says', replied Arthur, 'that the sun will rise over Almscliff Crag, as viewed from the Cow and Calf, twice a year. The next one's on the Seventh of September. That's three days from now.'

Ginny studied the copy of the parchment.

'I've got it!' she cried. 'Somehow, we've got to find a cup and a ring and then stand on either Almscliff Crag, or the Cow and Calf, I'm not sure which, three days from now.'

'That's what I reckon,' said Arthur.

'Do you know what, Arthur? I've just realised that day is Thursday!' exclaimed Ginny.

'So what?' said Arthur.

'The old name for Thursday is Thor's Day,' explained Ginny, 'It all fits in. Don't you see?'

Arthur nodded. Ginny looked excited.

'Arthur?' she queried. 'Do you think this might stop Albert Lockey building on the Moor and knocking down Folfoot Farm as well?'

'It could all be tied in,' confirmed Arthur. 'I think the first thing we've got to do is go out to the Doubler Stones. Then we'll see.'

'I don't suppose any of this will help Dad,' Ginny said sadly.

'I don't think we can do anything for him,' said Arthur, shaking his head, locking his hands between his knees, and staring at the floor.

Just then, there was a knock on the bedroom door. Ginny opened it, and it was Leonard.

'Your bikes 'ave coom,' he said. 'I don't know what you're doin' skulkin' in your room on a day like this.'

The children had been so deep in conversation that they had not heard Leonard coming back from the station in the trap with their bikes.

'We're thinking of going over to the Doubler Stones, today,' said Arthur.

'Oh! I haven't bin over there for years,' commented Leonard. 'I suppose you'll be wantin' sandwiches? I'll get Molly to meck you soom.'

The children went downstairs to look at their bicycles. Leonard had put them in an old lean-to shed by the shippon. They were none the worse for their journey. They were both mountain bikes, and Arthur's was in shades of blue, whereas Ginny's was in pink. The children took them out of the shed and tried them out around the farmyard, riding them through all the puddles. They left them propped up against the farmhouse. They then collected their sandwiches from Molly, and Arthur packed them in his rucksack. He noticed the broken flask in the bag, left over from the day before. He went to Molly with the flask.

'I'm sorry, Molly,' he apologised, 'but I had an accident on the Moor with this flask.'

He held out the flask. Molly took it and shook it.

'Oh,' she said when she realised that the flask was broken. 'It don't matter. We'll get a refill for this one. And we've got anoother. I suppose you'll be wantin' that one filled with 'ot water?'

Arthur said, 'Yes,' and apologised again. Molly boiled the kettle and filled another flask, giving it to Arthur, who packed it in his bag. Before Arthur and Ginny started out, Arthur borrowed a small green-and-red trowel that he had seen in the shed. He packed it in his bag.

'We may need this,' he said to Ginny.

The children set off by a route that they knew well by now. Reaching the Addingham bypass, they followed a sign to the left that said Addingham Moorside. The ground was rising and falling in front of them as they went along on their bicycles. Pigeons flew up into the air from the road. They crossed a stream that sparkled and shone in the morning light. Soon, they began to climb. It was hard work, despite the low gears that they had on their bikes. Eventually, they reached a crossroad. There was a milestone to the right with To Otley 10 Mls written on it. To the left was a prominent sign, saying Straight Lane.

'Do we turn off here, Arthur?' demanded Ginny.

Arthur studied the map.

'No, we want the next on the left. Lightbank Lane,' replied Arthur.

The children rested here for a while and then carried on down a hill and turned into Lightbank Lane. The road went uphill again. There were a couple of young girls out riding some horses. The children waved to the girls as they passed them. Now, there were some small crags above the children. The town of Silsden spread below them. Eventually, the road came to a sharp corner, and turned right downhill. The children continued to the left up a concrete farm track. Coming to the top of the hill and passing through a gate, they could see a ridge in front of them.

Below the ridge, there were the remains of a small quarry, and there was an unoccupied bungalow below that. There was a very strange-looking stone on the horizon. It looked rather like a mushroom with the central part of it eaten away.

'That looks like one of the Doubler Stones, Arthur!' cried Ginny, pointing.

As Arthur and Ginny were approaching the bungalow, they spotted the figure of the geologist by the side of the track. They stopped their bikes. He came over to them.

'Still looking for your hammer?' enquired Arthur.

'I think I will have to get another,' the geologist replied.

'You're nothing to do with the Ilkley town mayor, are you?' asked Ginny.

'No. You might say that we are enemies,' said the geologist, smiling.

'Are the Doubler Stones up there?' Ginny continued, pointing at the ridge.

'Yes. You will find them at the top of yon ridge. There are but two of them,' the geologist answered.

Arthur looked at his watch.

'I'm sorry, but we'll have to be moving,' he said.

The geologist bid them farewell. The children continued on their way.

'He's got a strange accent!' observed Ginny. 'Do you think he's some sort of a Scandinavian, Arthur?'

'Looks more like a Viking to me!' commented Arthur.

They went past the bungalow, to the right-hand side of the ridge, and up behind to a rise on the far side. The children could now see the two stones.

Ginny looked down over the edge of the ridge to where the geologist had been. He had disappeared completely, just as he had done at the Barmishaw Stone.

'Stranger and stranger!' thought Ginny.

They left their bikes chained up in the grass and went over to the two stones. The left-hand stone was the smaller of the two. Both stood about a head high and were about two metres across. The children guessed that the reason for their mushroom shape was the way they had been weathered. Arthur got on top of the left-hand stone. He found cup and ring marks on top of it. He could not get on to the right-hand stone. It was too high.

'Well', said Ginny, 'we have to look for a ring somewhere at the base of one of these stones. Is that right?'

Arthur agreed. He got out the trowel. They decided to start at the bottom of the left-hand stone. They began to probe around the stone. The stones were on a rock platform, and the soil was thin. Even so, there was a large area to cover. They found nothing at the base of the left-hand stone and started to investigate the right-hand stone. They scrabbled around for half an hour or so.

'It's no good,' said Ginny, finally. 'We'll never find anything here.'

Their nails were full of grit, and the knees of their jeans were covered with soil.

'We'll have a cup of tea and have a think,' said Arthur.

Arthur got out the new flask and some tea bags and dried milk left over from the day before. He made two cups of tea. The children sat gloomily on the edge of the ridge.

Suddenly, Ginny pointed.

'There's someone over there!' she exclaimed. 'We've got nothing to lose. Perhaps we can ask them for help!'

The Doubler Stones

Coming over the Moor was a short man, wearing a duffel coat and a deerstalker hat. The children waved to him. As he came over towards them, they could see that he had headphones over his head and carried some sort of contraption on a pole in front of him. He had strong glasses that looked like pebbles.

'W-W-What's awl the foos?' stuttered the man when he got near.

Ginny had an idea.

'Is that a metal detector?' she queried.

'A-A-Aye,' answered the man. 'I-I-I med it misen. Q-Q-Quite neat, don't you think?'

He lifted up the pole of the detector and inspected the contraption on the end, a look of pride on his face.

'I wonder if you could help us?' queried Ginny. 'My mother tells me that she lost a ring near here, when I was small. Would you be able to find it?'

'A-A-Aye,' replied the man. 'I-I-I don't really believe you, b-b-boot we'll 'ave a go.'

The man began sweeping the detector over the area near the stones. The children discovered that the man's name was Joe Grimshaw. He had walked up from Silsden to look for Roman coins and the like, but all he ever seemed to find were bits of silver foil from sweet wrappings.

Joe searched over all the places indicated by the children, but he found nothing. Finally, he rested the detector on the ground.

'Th-Th-There's nowt 'ere,' Joe said. 'Wh-Wh-What kind of a gemm are you l-l-lakin' at?'

He gave the detector an angry sweep low down near the ground.

"Ello?' he remarked. 'Wh-Wh-What's this!'

The detector had found something. He bent down with a trowel that he had, dug in the thin soil, and drew out something caked in mud. He cleaned it off with a rag. The children gathered anxiously around him, looking. It was a ring.

'W-W-Well, now,' observed Joe. 'I-I-If you weren't right, a-a-after all!'

He handed the Ring to Arthur. Arthur and Ginny looked at it. It did not look at all special. It did not have any decoration on it, or precious stones set in it, and looked as if it were made of brass.

'Is this it?' demanded Ginny.

'Looks like it,' confirmed Arthur.

Arthur popped it in the side pocket of his rucksack.

'What have we here?' said a voice.

It was the Police Officer that the children had met in Ilkley three days ago. They had been so interested in the discovery that they had not seen him coming up the Moor.

'N-N-Nowt, o-o-Officer,' answered Joe.

'Is that a metal detector?' the Police Officer queried.

'A-A-Aye,' replied Joe. 'W-W-What of it?'

'Do you have a licence to use that thing on the Moor?' the Police Officer boomed.

'N-N-No, Officer, I-I-I didn't know you needed one,' returned Joe, innocently.

'You know well enough that it is against County Bylaws to use metal detectors on Rombalds Moor without a licence,' intoned the Police Officer.

He turned to the children.

'Haven't I seen you before?' he asked.

'No. Never,' answered Arthur.

'Are you his children?' queried the Police Officer, nodding at Joe.

'Yes. We are,' lied Arthur.

'Then you're all coming along with me,' directed the Police Officer, 'We'll see what Albert Lockey has to say about this.'

They protested their innocence, but the hard-faced Officer would not listen to them. He had drawn up in a Police car, which was below on the concrete track. They reluctantly got into the car, and the Officer drove off. They passed the journey to Ilkley in silence. Halfway there, the children realised that they had left their bikes behind.

They pulled up outside the front of the town hall. They got out of the Police car. Joe left the metal detector in it. The Officer led them in through some swing doors, across an entrance hall, and up a flight of stairs at the far side. They climbed two flights of stairs to a landing with a wooden balustrade and turned left along a corridor. The Officer halted outside an office marked A. Lockey and knocked on the door. Through a glass panel in the door, they could see Albert Lockey. He came to the door, opened it, and the Officer explained to him what had happened. Albert Lockey looked furious. He bundled them in through the door and sat down at a desk, his fingers together at the tips. He did not offer them seats. The Officer was waiting outside.

'I suppose you know that this is a very serious offence?' he fumed. 'There are some very rare archaeological remains on the Moor. We don't want just anyone coming and disturbing them.'

'I-I-I belong to a N-N-National Society,' retorted Joe. 'W-W-We 'ave very strict guidelines. W-W-We don't take nowt without permission.'

'You didn't find anything up there, did you?' Albert Lockey asked slyly.

He seemed to lean forward in his seat in anticipation.

'Oh. N-N-Nowt. N-N-Nowt at a',' replied Joe, winking at the children when Albert Lockey was not looking.

'Are you sure about that?' pressed Albert Lockey.

'Wh-Wh-When I say nowt, I-I-I mean nowt,' returned Joe, crossing his fingers behind his back.

'Very well, then,' conceded Albert Lockey, falling back in his seat.

The children breathed a sigh of relief. Albert Lockey drew a piece of paper from the drawer of his desk. He started reading it out.

'Any person or persons found using metal detectors' he intoned, 'or any such similar devices on Rombalds Moor, or its environs, or digging in archaeological sites, without prior authorisation, shall be liable to a fine not exceeding . . .'

He turned the paper around and stabbed at an amount.

'I will, of course, give you a receipt,' he said, smiling thinly.

Joe dug into the pocket of his duffel coat and pulled out his wallet. He only just had enough money, which he handed over to Albert Lockey. Albert Lockey slipped out another piece of paper from the desk. He started writing furiously on it.

'Name?' he curtly asked Joe.

'J-J-Joe Evans,' answered Joe.

'Address?' Albert Lockey demanded.

Joe gave him an invented address in Silsden. Albert Lockey completed the form, signed it, and handed a carbon copy to Joe.

'These are your children, I presume?' Albert Lockey queried.

Joe confirmed that Arthur and Ginny were his children. Albert Lockey turned to them.

'Haven't I met you before?' he asked them.

'No. We've never seen you before,' replied Arthur, innocently.

'And what are your names?' Albert Lockey demanded.

'John and Jackie Evans,' returned Arthur, lying again.

Albert Lockey wrote down their names. He stood up behind the desk. He leaned towards the children, his hands spread out on top of the desk. His face contorted with anger.

'If I catch you making any more trouble on the Moor', he stormed, 'you won't know what hit you. Understand?'

The children nodded in silence, cowed by his wrath. Joe stepped forward and put a protective arm around the children.

'Y-Y-You leave my children alone,' he commanded. 'N-N-Now you've 'ad your say, w-w-we'll be needin' a lift 'ome.'

'How you get home is none of my concern,' Albert Lockey raged.

'N-N-Now see 'ere', instructed Joe, waving his finger at Albert Lockey, 'I-I-I've 'ad just about enough o' you. N-N-Now I've paid t' fine with my own brass, I-I-I expect better treatment than this.'

Albert Lockey slapped the top of the desk with both hands.

'Very well, then', he shouted, 'I'll get the Officer outside to take you all back to Silsden, if that's what you want.'

Arthur thought quickly.

'Dad, here, lives in Silsden', he explained, 'but we live in Ben Rhydding with our mother. It's not far. We'll walk.'

With hardly a word more, Albert Lockey led them back into the corridor. He gruffly explained to the waiting Police Officer what was wanted. They were led outside to the Police car, and Joe got in. The Police Officer started up the engine.

'We'll pay you back someday, Dad!' cried the children, as the car pulled away.

When the Police car had gone, Arthur looked around. There was nobody about. He started dancing in the middle of the pavement.

'We've got the Ring! We've got the Ring!' he sang.

'Shhh,' directed Ginny, her fingers to her lips, 'Do you want everyone to know?'

When Arthur had calmed down, they went along to the fountain at the head of Brook Street, and sat down.

'That was a close shave!' Arthur observed. 'If we're not careful, Albert Lockey will be on to us.'

Ginny started.

'What about our bikes?' she said.

'We'll have to pick them up some other day,' Arthur stated, 'They're OK. They're chained up. I don't think we'll have the time to go back, anyway.'

He got the Ring out of his rucksack to study it in more detail.

'It looks very ordinary,' commented Ginny. 'Are you sure this is it?'

'Looking at it, now, I'm not so sure,' replied Arthur. 'But I think we're going to soon find out.'

He retrieved the copy of the parchment from his bag. He read out the third verse.

Maiden, wear ye Ring,
Maiden, drink Wine from ye Cup,
Stand thou on ye Badger,
When ye Full moon is just up,

'The way I see it, Gin,' he explained, 'is that we've got to be up at the Badger Stone at the next full moon. We'll also need some wine.'

Arthur consulted his diary.

'There's a full moon on Wednesday,' he stated. 'We're going to have to find the Cup before then. I told you we haven't much time.'

'But do we know what time the moon rises?' Ginny asked.

Arthur studied his diary again.

'The sun sets at about seven forty-five on Wednesday', he remarked, 'and if I've got my science right, the full moon rises shortly after that. I don't know in what direction, though.'

'About the wine', Ginny continued, 'we'll never be able to buy any. We're too young.' She thought for a moment. 'I've got it!' she cried. 'I've remembered that Len makes his own wine. There are some bottles of it in the kitchen.'

'Good!' Arthur concluded. 'We're all set. Tomorrow, we'll try and find Jim. I think he'll work out the second verse.'

They put everything back in Arthur's rucksack and cautiously made their way back to the farm. They glanced back along the road from time to time, to make sure that nobody was following them. As they were approaching the farm, they realised that the Dickinsons would expect them to have their bikes with them. When they got into the farmyard, they made a point of going into the shed and loudly slamming the door. Arthur put the trowel back. Neither Leonard nor Molly noticed anything amiss. The children made arrangements to go up to the Cow and Calf the next day.

A nearly full moon rose over the Moor that night. It was going to be a harvest moon.

CHAPTER EIGHT

The Twelve Apostles

There was a mist on the Moor. Dewdrops formed on the heather and dripped on to the peat. The bedraggled sheep huddled together for warmth. All over, there was a deadening silence, punctuated only by the lonely cry of the curlew.

Ginny woke first, long before the alarm was due to go off. She was still intrigued by the Ring. She had got it out of Arthur's rucksack and was toying with it, moving it from finger to finger. All of a sudden, there was a dreadful commotion from the farmyard.

Ginny looked out of the window. A young bullock had got free from the shippon. It was chasing around the farmyard, bucking, kicking, and bellowing. Leonard was trying to slip a halter around its neck and shouting to Molly. Molly was trying to head it off, her apron flapping. Jess was barking furiously, running around the farmyard and getting in the way. Arthur was woken by the noise.

'What's happening?' he asked.

'A bullock has got free down in the farmyard. Let's go down and help,' Ginny answered.

The children slipped on their nightgowns and slippers and made their way down to the front door. They swung open the front door and Ginny stepped out. The bullock caught sight of Ginny and a strange change came over it. It stood rooted to the spot, staring out of round eyes. Then, it walked quietly over to Ginny, snorting. Ginny put out her hand to touch its snout. The bullock's front legs collapsed on to the ground. Ginny knelt down on her haunches. With a weird lowing sound, the bullock laid its head in Ginny's lap, its eyes rolling. Leonard easily slipped the halter around the bullock's neck.

'Well!' Leonard exclaimed. 'If that don't beat all!'

He led the docile bullock away to the shippon. Ginny stared down at her left hand. The Ring was on it. Arthur was standing next to her.

'Could it be this ring?' queried Ginny, holding up the Ring.

'I don't know,' Arthur replied. 'But perhaps you'd better not wear it again until Wednesday night.'

Arthur put the Ring away in a drawer in their bedroom for safe keeping.

The children washed, got dressed, and had breakfast. Arthur replenished his supply of tea bags and dried milk and got the usual sandwiches and flask of hot water from Molly. Arthur found the trowel again. The children got ready to go.

'We're off up to the Cow and Calf,' Arthur told Molly when they were ready.

'You never seem to be off t' Moor,' commented Molly. 'There's plenty of things to do in t' town, you know.'

'We'd rather be on the Moor,' explained Arthur.

The children trooped out into the farmyard, and were walking away, when Molly shouted out from the kitchen.

'Aren't you usin' your bikes?' she called.

Arthur looked embarrassed.

'We don't need them. We're coming back across the Moor,' he called back.

'Mind you, look out in all this mist,' Molly concluded.

The children continued into the town. Cheeky blackbirds mocked the unearthly silence. Their footsteps echoed hollowly down the street. When they got into the town, there was hardly anyone about, it being a Tuesday. The children passed quickly along the Grove and then got a shock on passing Brook Street. There were many people lining the street, and a procession was passing up it. There was a brass band marching, and the children saw many banners. One read,

JESUS SAVES—SAVE THE MOOR,

and another read,

FOR GOD'S SAKE, STOP DEVELOPMENT ON THE MOOR.

The marchers were handing out stickers and badges. At the head of the procession, the children recognised Madeleine English. She spotted them in the crowd and came over.

'I thought it was you!' she cried. 'Are you going to help us stop Albert Lockey?'

Ginny nodded and then said, 'We have our own plans to beat Albert Lockey, Madeleine!'

Madeleine looked puzzled and was about to say something, but was called back to the procession. The children melted into the crowd and continued on their way. They slid quickly past the town hall and up the road out of the town. When they got to the beck, instead of going over the cattle grid, they went through a gate and up the beck. It was a tough climb to the top. They continued past the eastern end of Rocky Valley, where there was a ford, and went further up the beck. Despite the mist, they could see for about half a mile up here. They had only the murmur of the water for company. When they rounded the corner where the dead sheep had been, Arthur suddenly pulled Ginny down into the bracken.

'Get down!' he cried.

They peered through the bracken. There were two Policemen up at the ruined building. They were wandering around, prodding Jim's few scant possessions with their boots and discussing something together.

'Pssst,' sounded something.

'Is that an adder?' said Ginny, looking slightly alarmed.

'Pssst,' sounded something again.

There was a rustling in the bracken, and a head popped through to where the children were hiding. It was Jim.

'Jim!' whispered Arthur. 'There you are! We thought the Police had got you.'

'It'll take more than a few Policemen to get me off this Moor,' Jim vowed.

They all looked up to the ruined building. The Policemen had gone.

'Jim,' said Arthur, 'we haven't much time. Do you know what this means?'

He took out the copy of the parchment and read out the second verse.

> Twelve sat down,
> At ye Last Feast,
> Look thou Inside me,
> And find ye Cup of Peace.

Jim looked worried and started shaking, just as he had done two days before.

'Twelve and thirteen,' he cackled. 'There were thirteen once. Jesus is the Bridge! Jesus is the Way! Jesus is Lord!'

'Do you know what he means?' Arthur asked Ginny.

'I think he's talking about Jesus and the twelve disciples,' observed Ginny.

'That's it!' cried Arthur. 'The Twelve Apostles! They're here on the map. They're not far. We can go there straight away.'

Arthur showed the map to Ginny. She looked at it and then looked at Jim. She noticed that he was looking very distressed.

'What about Jim?' Ginny commented.

Arthur looked at Jim and saw the state he was in.

'I'm very sorry, Jim,' Arthur apologised, 'but we had to work out the riddle. Do you want a cup of tea?'

'I've got no paraffin left for the Primus,' Jim whimpered.

'It's all right,' consoled Arthur, pulling out the flask. 'We've got some hot water here.'

They all went up to the ruin. Jim lay down on his bed while Arthur made two cups of tea. Jim and Arthur shared one of the cups. Ginny asked Arthur to get out a bar of chocolate that Molly had packed, and they shared that. After a while, Jim looked very much happier.

'What are you going to do about the Police?' Ginny asked Jim.

'They won't catch me!' he sniggered. 'I've got a few tricks up my sleeve. Don't you worry about me.'

'What about the paraffin?' enquired Arthur.

'Oh, I'll get some more,' Jim answered. 'I've got some money. Don't worry about that.'

'So you're OK?' queried Ginny, feeling concerned about him.

'I'll be all right,' concluded Jim.

Arthur and Ginny decided that they had better be moving on. They packed up their things, said goodbye to Jim, and started up the beck. They soon hit the track to Rocky Valley and turned the other way, further into the heart of the Moor. Sodden sheep dotted the landscape.

There was someone coming towards them through the mist. The children looked for somewhere to hide, but the Moor was barren at this point. Then, they recognised the person. It was the geologist.

'Well met!' exclaimed the geologist when he had come up to the children.

'What are you doing up here?' asked Arthur.

'I am always about this Moor,' replied the geologist.

'Where do you come from?' enquired Ginny. 'Aren't you far from home?'

'I come from Belskirnir in Thrudvang,' the geologist answered. 'It is very far from here. But are you not looking for something?'

'We're looking for the Twelve Apostles,' returned Arthur. 'Are they near here?'

'The Twelve Apostles are beyond the Lanshaw Lad on the next ridge,' the geologist replied, pointing. 'But now, much as I would continue talking with you, I must continue with my quest for my hammer, so I will bid you farewell.'

The geologist made a courtly bow to the children and then went off into the mist.

'I've never heard of a town called Belskirnir or a country called Thrudvang,' commented Ginny when the geologist was out of sight.

'He seems obsessed with his hammer too,' observed Arthur.

The children continued following the path across the Moor. Coming up to another ridge, a rectangular, roughly cut stone stood out of the mist.

'That'll be the Lanshaw Lad,' commented Arthur, studying the map. 'The Twelve Apostles should be somewhere near here.'

They carried on and saw a collection of small, strangely shaped stones in the heather to their left.

'That'll be it!' exclaimed Arthur. 'It's a stone circle!'

They walked over to the stone circle. It was in a state of disrepair. Some of the stones had fallen over and had been propped up again. Ginny counted the stones out loud, pointing at each one. There were twelve of them. It was apparent that someone had already been digging in the circle.

'Albert Lockey?' questioned Ginny, pointing to the holes in the ground.

'Possibly,' returned Arthur.

Arthur turned to Ginny.

'You agree that we have to look somewhere in this circle for a cup?' he asked.

Ginny nodded.

'Then I'm going to use my dowsing rods,' he continued, getting the rods out of his rucksack.

'Not those, Arthur,' Ginny said in dismay. 'You heard what Madeleine English said.'

'Well, how else are we going to find the Cup?' Arthur replied. 'It could be buried deep underground, for all we know, and we don't have Joe Grimshaw's metal detector to help us.'

'Oh, all right', conceded Ginny. 'But you be careful.'

Arthur proceeded to wander backwards and forward across the circle, holding out the rods. When he was going towards the centre of the circle, they appeared to cross and uncross every few feet.

'It's no good,' he observed. 'I'm getting the charged fields inside this circle. I'll have to concentrate on a cup. Pity we don't know what it's made of.'

Arthur started surveying the circle again. The reaction of the rods changed as he concentrated. He was getting no response anywhere. Finally, near the largest stone in the circle, the rods crossed. He dug the trowel into the ground. He approached the spot from a different direction. The rods crossed again.

'I've found something!' shouted Arthur.

Ginny came over to the place.

'Is this where the Cup is?' she asked.

'I think so,' answered Arthur.

'How do we know how deep it is?' Ginny queried.

'That's easy,' replied Arthur. 'We'll use the Bishop's Rule.'

'The Bishop's Rule?' enquired Ginny.

'Haven't you ever read any of the books on dowsing by Tom Graves?' Arthur questioned.

'No,' returned Ginny. 'Who's Tom Graves?'

'Really!' Arthur remarked. 'First you haven't heard of Alfred Watkins, and now you haven't heard of Tom Graves. Honestly, your depth of ignorance totally astounds me.'

'I'm as clever as you,' Ginny retorted. 'I can do anything you can do, and someday I could have a baby. You try and do that!'

Ginny stood there defiantly, her arms crossed. Her lower lip trembled. Arthur put his hand on her shoulder.

'I'm sorry, Gin,' he apologised. 'I didn't mean to upset you. I'll show you the Bishop's Rule.'

Arthur turned around, went back to the trowel, and started to shuffle slowly away from it. He held the dowsing rods out in front of him. About half a metre from the trowel, the rods crossed.

'It's half a metre underground,' Arthur stated.

Something was happening to the stones. They were becoming blurred and seemed to be multiplying.

'How many were there?' Arthur thought. 'Surely there are more than twelve.'

Arthur started to count them.

'One... two... three...'

He lost count. He started again.

'One... two... three... four...'

The stones were crowding in on Arthur. Strange figures in animal skins with their faces painted with ochre in strange patterns were approaching him. They were holding out branches of mistletoe, dancing in an odd way and chanting in a language that Arthur did not understand. The figures gathered in a circle around Arthur, swaying from side to side. One of them held some mistletoe over his head, while another pressed a berry to his lips. An awful taste came into Arthur's mouth. It was choking him. His head whirled around and around. The sky was turning black. There was a buzzing noise in Arthur's ears.

Arthur's knees buckled under him. He dropped the dowsing rods. He collapsed unconscious to the ground. Blood trickled from his nose.

Ginny had seen what was happening to Arthur. She came running over. She knew what to do, as she had studied first aid at school. There was only a little blood coming from his nose. She wiped it up with her handkerchief. Next, she checked that he had not been sick, that his breathing passages were free, and that his breathing was normal. She checked his pulse. She then reached into Arthur's Cagjack pocket and pulled out a pill case. She opened it and selected a capsule from inside. It was yellow at one end, and clear at the other, with little blue and white bobbles visible inside it. It looked like a multicoloured bullet. She took a cup and the flask from Arthur's rucksack. She put a little water in the Cup and put the capsule in Arthur's mouth, whilst getting him to drink the water. He coughed and swallowed the capsule.

Ginny put Arthur in the recovery position and sat holding his hand. She knew that it was not a good idea to leave Arthur and try to find help. She put her anorak over Arthur's shoulders and tried calling out 'Help!' from time to time. The mist swallowed her cries.

After a quarter of an hour, Arthur's eyes flickered. He saw Ginny.

'Oh, Ginny,' he murmured. 'What happened?'

'You've just had one of your turns,' answered Ginny. 'Just lie still till you feel better.'

Arthur closed his eyes. The colour was returning to his face. After another quarter of an hour, he groaned and sat up.

'All the stones seemed to be crowding in on me,' he quavered. 'I saw strange men here.'

'Oh, Arthur,' Ginny reproached, 'you shouldn't go dowsing in stone circles. Specially if you're not quite right in the head and after what everyone's been saying.'

'I won't do it again,' promised Arthur.

Arthur's strength was returning by the minute. He picked up the fallen dowsing rods, and put them in his rucksack, vowing never to use them again. He stood up shakily and stretched his legs.

'Now, we've got to dig for the Cup,' he said.

'Are you sure you're all right?' queried Ginny.

'I'll be fine,' replied Arthur.

They proceeded to dig at the point indicated by the trowel. The peat was soggy and the hole kept filling up with water. Finally, the trowel scraped against something. Arthur reached into the hole and pulled at an object. It came out of the hole with a sucking noise. He cleaned it with his handkerchief. It was a cup.

The children examined the Cup. It was small, brown, and earthenware. It was slightly cracked and chipped. It had had a handle once, but it had long since been broken off. It was totally plain, having no decoration on it at all.

'This looks just as ordinary as the Ring,' commented Ginny.

'Yes,' said Arthur. 'And Joe's metal detector wouldn't have found this.'

There was a shout behind them. Two men had come up past the Lanshaw Lad, and were running towards the stone circle.

'Run for it!' shouted Arthur, grabbing his rucksack and stuffing the Cup into it.

The children ran off down the Moor, the men following in hot pursuit. The heather was like a spongy mattress under the children's pounding feet. The mist was coming down and making it hard for the men to follow. The children came down into a large hollow in the hillside, where the men could not see, and dived into some thick bracken. The men stood at the top of the hollow.

'Where do we find them in that lot?' one man asked.

'We've got to find the little shavers,' replied the other.

The men began searching around in the hollow, stamping the bracken down. They searched for half an hour. Eventually, they were within a couple of yards of the place where the children were hiding.

'It's no good,' the first man said. 'We'll never find them in this mist and in all this bracken. They could be anywhere on this hillside. They could even have got away by now.'

'You're right,' agreed the other. 'We'll just have to report back.'

The men went back up towards the Twelve Apostles, and Arthur and Ginny let go the breath that they had been holding.

The children waited for the men to get well away and then stealthily made their way back to the Twelve Apostles. Ginny retrieved their flask and cups, which they had abandoned in their haste. The children crept up to the top of the ridge, near the Lanshaw Lad, and looked out over the Moor. For as far as they could see in the mist, there was no one about. They discussed things and decided to make their way back to Folfoot Farm over the top of the Moor.

They travelled to the western end of Rocky Valley but instead of going down the steps, turned left. Arthur was having trouble navigating in the mist. Despite his map and compass, they started going back into the heart of the Moor. They had to retrace their steps, and, only then, did they strike a path going in the right direction. The Moor was lonely up here. It seemed to roll on in the mist endlessly. Old stones stood in dark, dank pools of peaty water. Small birds flitted silently from tussock to tussock. Ginny felt sorry for the poor, drenched sheep. They occasionally disturbed one, which got up begrudgingly from the dry ground it had been lying on. Arthur was not so sympathetic.

'You know that they invented a computer program to translate from English into Russian and another to translate back again?' he said to Ginny.

'I've got a feeling a dreadful joke is coming up,' answered Ginny.

'Well,' continued Arthur, 'they put in "hydraulic ram", translated it into Russian, and back again. You know what they got out?'

'I dread to think,' replied Ginny.

'A "wet sheep"!' Arthur crowed triumphantly, pointing to one of the sheep.

'Very funny, I don't think,' answered Ginny. 'At least you're back to normal after the trouble at the Twelve Apostles.'

The children walked on in silence and then spotted a man coming over the Moor. They instantly recognised him. It was Joe Grimshaw. He had his metal detector with him.

"Ee 'ello!' he said when he had drawn near. 'Wh-Wh-What are you doin' oop 'ere!'

'We could very well ask you the same question, Joe,' answered Ginny.

'Oh,' replied Joe. 'I-I-I'm not bothered by that idiot A-A-Albert Lockey. I-I-I'll still coom oop on t' Moor, wh-wh-whatever 'e says.'

'We're not bothered by him either,' commented Arthur. 'By the way, what's your address?'

'Wh-Wh-Why do you want to know that?' queried Joe.

'So we can pay you back the money you handed over to Albert Lockey,' returned Arthur.

'That b-b-brass?' snorted Joe. 'D-D-Don't you woorry about the brass. I-I-It were worth it, t-t-to sneak that ring out f-f-from oonder that f-f-fool's nose. Y-Y-you've still got it?'

'Yes', answered Arthur, 'but it's at home.'

'Y-Y-Your moother got it back?' queried Joe.

Arthur looked a little shamefaced.

'Yes, Joe,' he replied, 'she got it back.'

'G-G-Good!' exclaimed Joe. 'W-W-Well, you're going t' oother way to me, s-s-so we'll say "Goodbye". N-N-No doubt we'll meet on t' Moor agen.'

With that, Joe was away. He soon disappeared into the mist. The children carried on and came upon the Badger Stone, almost without realising it.

Arthur and Ginny were very hungry by now. They sat down on the bench by the Stone, and had their sandwiches and tea. Flies were pestering them unmercifully, but they were too hungry to care. After their meal, Arthur got out the Cup from his bag. There was nothing to distinguish it from anything you could buy in a second-hand shop, for a few pence. Ginny took it from Arthur.

'So I have to stand on top of the Badger Stone with it, like this,' she commented, going over to the Badger Stone, and balancing on top, her legs on either side of the ridge.

'I can hear something coming from the Stone!' exclaimed Arthur.

He put his ear to the Stone. A deep humming noise seemed to be coming from it.

Ginny listened. She got down from the Stone. The sound had gone away.

'Don't be silly!' she reproached Arthur. 'On top of everything else, Arthur, you hear things.'

The children packed up their things and moved off. Instead of going over the Moor straight to the Swastika Stone, they decided to go down the moorside and over to Heber's Ghyll. They had realised that no one was going to see them in the mist. As they neared Barmishaw Wood, a rabbit hopped off into the undergrowth. The mist hung like shrouds in the wood.

They got slightly lost coming down the slope and ended up wading through bracken. Their legs got very wet. Arthur's boots were full of water by this time and were sloshing.

They got down to the Keighley Road. There were rowan trees here, with their crimson berries seeming to glow in the mist. They found an unmade road leading to Heber's Ghyll and followed it. After a while, they crossed the bridge at the head of Heber's Ghyll, and, from there, made their way up to the Swastika Stone.

'The hammer of Thor!' commented Arthur, looking through the railings at the Swastika. 'I'm sure that Thor is bound up with this, somehow.'

They had a little water left in the flask, with which they made a last cup of tea. They then went down to Folfoot Farm.

'It were a moocky day on t' Moor,' observed Leonard that evening, when they were sitting down to tea.

'We think the Moor is marvellous at any time, Len,' retorted Ginny.

'I'm gettin' a bit woories about you two spendin' all your time on t' Moor,' remarked Leonard.

'Don't you think we're quite used to the Moor, by now, Len?' replied Ginny.

'Appen', concluded Leonard, 'you joost watch out, that's all.'

Leonard was about to continue with his tea, when he remembered something. He looked pleased.

'Oh!' he beamed. 'There's soom good news for you! I heard on t' radio that the UN are negotiatin' for your father's release and they're mekin' progress.'

The children were relieved to hear the news.

They were continuing with their tea, when there was a knock at the door. Leonard let his knife and fork go with a clatter.

'Oo's disturbin' good farmin' folk, while their 'avin' their tea?' he muttered.

Leonard answered the door. It was two Policemen.

'Good evening, Mr Dickinson,' said one of the Policemen. 'I'm Constable Hawksworth, and this is Constable Parkinson.'

The Policemen showed their identity cards.

'We were just doing some investigations in this area,' continued the Officer. 'We wondered, do a John and Jackie Evans live here?'

'There's no one 'ere by that name,' replied Leonard, quite truthfully.

'Well, if you hear of them, they've been creating a good deal of nuisance on the Moor,' persisted the Officer.

'I'll keep a look out for them. And now, if you don't mind, I've got to be about my business,' Leonard concluded.

He closed the door. Leonard came back into the living room. There were sounds of doors slamming and a car driving away.

'Don't troost t' Police around 'ere,' Leonard said, scratching his neck.

He turned to the children.

'You two bin oop to owt on t' Moor?' he queried.

'No. We've been very well behaved,' replied Ginny, looking innocent.

'Well', continued Leonard, staring intently at the children, 'if I 'ear of owt, I'm not lettin' you out on t' Moor agen.'

Night was falling on the Moor. There was an inconclusive sunset, but towards midnight, the skies started to clear from the west. A blood-red moon set over the far horizon in the west. The Moor was waiting.

CHAPTER NINE

The Badger Stone Revisited

The children were woken by a rhythmic hacking noise. They looked out of the bedroom window. Leonard was in the yard, cutting wood for the fire. His strong arms rose and fell, and the wood splintered. The sun beamed on to the stone of the farm, making it look warm and golden. The light streamed through the window, illuminating the colours of the children's counterpanes. 'What a change from yesterday!' thought the children. They sat in bed and discussed what they needed to do next. Arthur had got hold of a copy of *Whitaker's Almanack* that the Dickinsons had. He confirmed that the moon would rise shortly after the sun set that evening. Arthur and Ginny decided to wait at the farm until then.

The children washed, dressed, and had breakfast. They told Molly that they had decided to stay at the farm that day. She had discovered their handkerchiefs.

'You're a reet couple of moocky poops,' she said, inspecting the handkerchiefs. 'Where's all the blood coom from?'

'It's Arthur,' replied Ginny. 'He gets these funny turns, now and then. He's better now. It doesn't happen very often.'

Molly looked concerned but made no further comment. Leonard came in from the farmyard, taking off his boots.

'Mash us a coop of tea, Moother,' he said.

Molly hurried off into her kitchen. Leonard came into the living room. He looked surprised.

'I thought as 'ow you'd be oop on t' Moor, by now,' he observed.

'We're staying, here, at the farm, today,' replied Ginny.

'It'll meck a change, any road,' returned Leonard. 'I'll tell you what. In a little while from now, I'm goin' oop to t' top field to mend a broken wall. Do you want to coom along?'

'That'd be great!' answered the children.

Molly came back into the living room with Leonard's tea. He sat down at the table and started to drink it. They chatted for a while. Apparently, the farm was not doing so well. Getting things to market was a problem because of the petrol rationing, and he was not getting a good price for his produce. The government had also reduced and taken away any subsidies that they used to get.

'I'll tell thee, there's an endangered species oop t' Dales', said Leonard ruefully, scratching his head, 'and that's the Yorkshire Dales hill farmer!'

Leonard told them some more of his woes. He was worried about what would happen when he was much older and would not have the strength to look after the farm properly. There was no son to carry on with the business, and young men were discouraged at every turn from taking up farming. Eventually, he would have to live off his pension and let the farm go to rack and ruin. Leonard drained the last of his tea.

'Oh, well,' he sighed, slapping his knees and standing up with a grunt. 'I'll carry on while I've got t' strength in me—that is, if Albert Lockey'll let me. Now, then, you two, look sharp, we're off to mend a wall!'

Arthur's walking boots were still wet from the day before. He put on a pair of spare wellingtons that Leonard had. They were several sizes too large. Arthur, Ginny, and Leonard started up the track to the Moor. Where there had been an eerie silence the day before, there was the sound of birds twittering and cattle lowing. They looked back at the valley, spread below them. It was bathed in sunlight. Stretches of the river, visible to them, shone in the sunshine. They reached a field and climbed over a stile, and Leonard took the children to a stretch of broken wall.

'I started on this yesterday,' he said.

There was a pile of stones near the wall. Leonard started working. The children watched as he carefully selected each stone from the pile and gradually built up the wall.

'In the days when t' motor cars were runnin', he commented over his shoulder, whilst working, 'there were a stretch of wall over at Robin 'ole, by a sharp corner, that kept on bein' knocked down. T' local dry stonewaller refused to work on it, after a while. It used to near breck 'is 'eart to see 'is work bein' wasted.'

Arthur and Ginny sat on their cagoules and watched him for a while and then made their way back to the farm. Molly was in the kitchen when they got back.

'Is there anything we can help you with, Molly?' asked Ginny.

'As a matter of fact, there is,' replied Molly. 'You can go in t' garden and pick us soom goosegogs.'

Molly gave the children a large, white, china bowl. There was a small kitchen garden beyond the outhouse. The children went into it. There was a scent of herbs and flowers. A late butterfly fluttered from bloom to bloom. They spotted the gooseberry bushes and proceeded to pick the berries. They took care not to prick their fingers on the bushes but still got some prickles in them. They took the berries back to Molly in the kitchen.

'Just look at the gooseberries we've picked!' exclaimed Arthur, holding out the bowl.

'Aye,' said Molly, laughing. 'And, now that you've picked them, you can top an' tail them an' all!'

She handed the children two pairs of scissors and another bowl. Molly showed them what to do. They sat outside in the sunshine and got on with their task. Presently, Molly brought them some bread and cheese for lunch.

'What's that hen doing, over there, pecking at all the other hens?' Ginny asked Molly.

'Oh', explained Molly, 'that's Bossy Boots. She's in charge.'

The children had their lunch and then finished off the last of the gooseberries. They took everything back to Molly, who was making some pastry.

'Well done, children!' she exclaimed, wiping some flour from her nose. 'What are you goin' to do with the rest o' your day?'

'We were thinking of writing some letters,' answered Arthur.

The children went upstairs and spent the rest of the afternoon writing cards and letters. They did not mention in any of them the strange things that had been happening to them. Arthur and Ginny both wrote a special letter to their mother.

Soon, it was teatime. They all sat down to tea and had gooseberry pie, still warm from the oven, for afters. Over tea, the children discovered that Leonard and Molly had been invited to a neighbouring farm for the evening. The children knew that they would have to get away from the farm without the Dickinsons' noticing, so they were quite pleased with the situation. The

Dickinsons offered to take the children along with them, but they said that they wanted to get an early night. Leonard and Molly were amazed when Arthur and Ginny went upstairs at six o'clock. The children pretended to go to bed but lay on their beds, fully clothed. They had had a tiring day out in the fresh air. They soon started to drift off to sleep.

Ginny woke with a start. She had been having a complicated nightmare in which the Badger Stone had opened up and was swallowing her. She frantically inspected her watch. Thankfully, it was only a quarter to seven, but Ginny knew that they would have to hurry. She shook Arthur awake. They quietly opened the door to their bedroom. They heard Leonard and Molly going out. The children got the Cup and Ring from their hiding places and put them in Arthur's rucksack. Then they put on their nylon walking jackets and tiptoed downstairs. Arthur got a half-empty bottle of wine from the kitchen. Leonard had been drinking a little wine at tea. Molly had put newspaper in Arthur's boots, and they were now reasonably dry. They put on their boots and opened the front door.

The sun was on its way down. Straggling clouds were drifting by, high up in the sky. It was still quite light, but the farmyard was half in darkness due to a small wood to the west. The children stepped out into the farmyard. The Dickinsons could be seen, making their way along the lane to the west. Jess came bounding up.

'Don't bark, Jess, there's a good girl!' pleaded Arthur.

She stood there, whining. Ginny patted her on the head. She seemed satisfied, and padded back to her kennel. She lay down and put her head on her paws. Arthur suddenly jumped.

'What's that!' he exclaimed.

'Where?' asked Ginny.

'In the shadow, over there!' whispered Arthur urgently, pointing.

'I can't see anything,' replied Ginny.

'I thought I saw an old man with a wispy grey beard and a cloak,' explained Arthur.

Ginny peered into the semi-darkness.

'There's nothing there,' returned Ginny. 'You're very jumpy tonight!'

Arthur listened. All that could be heard was the stamp of Bracken, kicking in the stable and the breathing of the cattle in the shippon.

'Len told us that he had seen the ghost of the original Leonard Dickinson once or twice at this farm,' Arthur explained. 'I think I've just seen a ghost!' He shivered violently.

Ginny put her arm around Arthur's shoulders. 'Now, you're not going to have another of your turns, are you, Arthur?' Ginny enquired, looking into Arthur's face.

'Now, you're not going to have another of your turns, are you Arthur?' Ginny enquired, looking into Arthur's face.

Arthur pulled himself together. He bit his lower lip. He tore himself out of Ginny's arms and walked a few paces away.

'I'll be all right, Gin,' he said falteringly, looking over his shoulder at Ginny. 'I may be a loony, but I can look after myself.'

Ginny moved over and patted her Arthur's shoulder.

'Well, we can't spend all evening hanging around here!' said Arthur, brightening. 'What did the headscarf say to the hat, Ginny?'

'I've got no idea at all, Arthur,' said Ginny, smiling and shaking her head.

'You go on a head, I'll hang around hair!' sniggered Arthur, punching the air, 'Come on! Let's go!'

The children started out of the farmyard towards the Swastika Stone. Arthur got a small flashlight out of one of the pockets of his Cagjack. Ginny sometimes wondered what else he had in his pockets. Suddenly, Ginger, the cat, was caught in the light. He hissed, and his eyes blazed. He had caught something. He growled and dragged it into the darkness behind a wall. The children continued on their way.

As the children went up the path on to the Moor, there was an early owl hooting from Heber's Ghyll. Ginny turned to Arthur.

'I still think we should tell Len and Molly, Arthur,' she said.

'Len and Molly. Len and Molly,' said Arthur, crossly. 'This is a fine time to change your mind. Shut up and keep moving.'

They reached the top. The darkness under the Scotch pines looked menacing. They got to the Swastika Stone. The crag stood out darkly against the indigo sky. A little wind sighed across the railings. There was a figure standing by the Stone. The children recognised it as that of Alison Green.

'Hello, Alison!' cried Ginny, coming over to her. 'What are you doing up here?'

Alison jumped a little.

'Oh, hello, children,' she said when she realised who they were. 'I just came up here to see the setting sun. Albert and I like to come up here sometimes.'

'You mean, Albert Lockey?' asked Ginny.

'Yes,' said Alison, dreamily.

'We think he's the most awful man we've ever met,' said Ginny, rashly.

Alison woke out of her dream. She began to look angry.

'Well, I'll tell you something, young lady', snapped Alison, waving her finger at Ginny, 'I think he's a wonderful man. I love him, and I hope to marry him.'

'I'm sorry I said that,' apologised Ginny.

Alison was still angry. She ignored Ginny's apology.

'And another thing,' she raged. 'Albert tells me there are two children making a nuisance of themselves on the Moor, and now I know who they are. I'm off to tell him.'

Despite all attempts made by the children to placate Alison, she stamped off down the Moor towards Heber's Ghyll. When she was out of sight, Arthur turned to Ginny.

'What do we do now, Ginny?' he said, raising his arms in a shrug.

'I guess we carry on,' Ginny replied, biting her lower lip.

By the light of the setting sun, the children made their way down on to the Keighley Road and, from there, all the way up to the Badger Stone. The sun was going down in a blaze of glory. It was getting cold up here. There was not a breath of wind, and their bodies cast long shadows across the Moor. The weird markings on the Badger Stone stood out from the rock.

Arthur and Ginny sat down on the bench and waited. Arthur got out a carton of fruit juice and a bar of Kendal Mint Cake from his rucksack. He always carried something for emergencies. They shared the snack. Ginny was worried about Albert Lockey.

'Alison is going to tell Albert Lockey. What if he tells the Police and they find us up here, Arthur?' she asked.

'They won't find us, Ginny,' answered Arthur soothingly. 'They'll be looking for us over at the Swastika Stone. We're miles away from there.'

It was getting dark. Stars were beginning to twinkle in the sky. A mist was forming low down near the ground. Arthur could make out the flickering light of a satellite tracking across the heavens. He grew quite philosophical. For all his technological advancement, he thought, man had made some disastrous mistakes in space.

Ginny spotted it. Coming over the ridge behind them was the orange form of the full moon. Arthur quickly got the Cup and the Ring from his rucksack and handed them to Ginny. He got out the bottle of wine, uncorked it, and poured some wine into the Cup. Ginny hesitated.

'Can't you do this, Arthur?' she pleaded.

'You're the maiden. You do it,' Arthur replied curtly.

Ginny reluctantly went over to the Badger Stone and balanced on top of it. She did not know which finger to put the Ring on, so she put it on the forefinger of her right hand. She started to drink the wine from the Cup. The children waited in anticipation. Nothing seemed to be happening. The wine was trickling down Ginny's front, from a crack in the Cup. The moon went behind a cloud.

'This is ridiculous. I feel like a fool,' Ginny said peevishly. 'It's nothing but a cracked, old cup and a brass curtain ring.'

She dragged the Ring off her finger and jumped down from the Stone, thrusting the Cup into Arthur's hands.

'Give it another go, Gin,' begged Arthur.

'Oh, all right', Ginny conceded, 'but if nothing happens, I'm going home.'

It was quite dark by now. Arthur put some more wine in the Cup and handed it back to Ginny. The moon came out again from behind a cloud. The Badger Stone stood out from a layer of mist close to the ground. Ginny went back and stood on the Stone. This time, without noticing, she put the Ring on the third finger of her left hand. She drank from the Cup.

'Uggh, it tastes like blood,' she commented.

There was a sharp crack. Ginny leapt down from the Stone as if given an electric shock. The children stared at the Stone. The markings on it were beginning to glow. There was a low humming noise and a sound like the tinkling of tiny bells. The sound and light grew in intensity. Suddenly, narrow beams of light stabbed out into the darkness in several directions from the Stone. Some of the beams went out to neighbouring stones. The children could see that the markings on them were also beginning to glow. The sound was getting louder, and the light was getting brighter. No one else knew what was happening. There was nobody on the Moor that night, apart from a lone runner, who liked to run on the Moor on moonlit nights and who wondered what on earth was going on.

By now, the markings on the Badger Stone were shining in blue, red, and green. The sound and light reached a crescendo. A line of light appeared along the ridge of the Badger Stone. There was a grating noise, and the Stone split open. Arthur peered nervously into the cleft. Inside, he saw a hammer-like object bathed in light. He guessed what he had to do. He reached into the Stone and pulled out the hammer. It stung his fingers. He dropped it on the ground. With a groan, the Stone snapped shut. The sound stopped abruptly and the light extinguished itself. The moon went behind a cloud.

The children were left alone on the Moor in the darkness.

CHAPTER TEN

A Meeting with Thor

There was a hunting horn sounding across the Moor. By the light of his flashlight, Arthur inspected the hammer. It looked as though it were made of iron, and it was very highly decorated. It looked exactly like the hammer that the children had seen Leonard and Molly worshipping. Arthur placed it carefully in his rucksack. Then, he took the Cup from Ginny, who was still wearing the Ring. He was just debating whether to put the Cup in his bag also, when the horn sounded nearer. Arthur put away his flashlight.

Over the rise, above which the moon was still rising, came four fair-haired women, galloping on pure white horses. The horses kicked up the low mist in swirls as they raced towards the children. The women were dressed in very strange garb. They were wearing silver breastplates and carried golden shields in their right hands and spears in their left. The points of the spears glinted in the moonlight. The loveliest of the four women was leading and blowing on a horn. About her neck was the most beautiful necklace the children had ever seen. Arthur and Ginny were very afraid. They tried to run away, Arthur slinging the rucksack over his shoulders, but the women were too quick for them. Strong arms lifted them bodily on to two of the horses. The horses thundered away towards the Swastika Stone. They followed a route known well to the children. The horses' hoofs struck sparks from the Keighley Road.

As they came over to the Swastika Stone, the children noticed a strange change had come over it. Gone were the railings and the barbed wire. Instead, the Stone was bathed in an unearthly green light. The Swastika itself was glowing brightly. A figure stood on the rock. He had red hair and a red beard and was muscular in build. On his head was a horned helmet, and about him was a red cloak. He wore a gauntlet on his right hand and carried a double-bladed axe in his left hand. The cloak seemed to be furling and unfurling in a breeze, but there was no wind on the Moor that night. The party reached the Stone, and the women deposited the children on the ground. The women seemed to do that just as easily as they had picked them up. The women waited as their horses pawed the ground and stamped.

The man on the stone turned to them. He started saying something in a strange language to them. The children caught the names Freya and Brynhild as the man addressed them. They gathered that Freya was the leader of the women. The man dismissed them with a wave of his hand and whirled his axe about his head.

The horses reared up on their hind legs, and then the women charged away across the Moor to the south-west. As they moved away, the horses' hoofs began to leave the ground, until the whole company was flying through the air. The man on the stone rested his axe on the rock.

'Who awakens the Valkyries from The Skirtful of Stones?' he queried in a voice like thunder.

He turned to the children. 'Two children, I see!' he exclaimed. 'And I have met you before!'

'And what are your names, children?' he asked.

'A-A-Arthur,' replied Arthur, falteringly.

'G-G-Guinevere,' answered Ginny, who was so frightened that she used her full name.

Arthur was not so frightened as Ginny. He recognised the man.

'Wh-Wh-Who are you?' he enquired. 'A-A-Are you the geologist?'

'Yes,' confirmed the man. 'I am the geologist. I take on many appearances for I am Thor!'

Thor stamped, and his eyes threw out sparks. His voice reverberated, and the children's teeth seemed to rattle. He stared down at the children. Arthur still had the Cup in his hand, and Ginny had the Ring on her finger. Thor saw them.

'And what have we here!' he remarked. 'It is well that you are called Arthur and Guinevere, for these are none other than the Grail of King Arthur and the ring of Queen Guinevere!'

Thor stared down. He saw how frightened the children looked. He stepped down from the stone. 'But you need not be so afraid!' he said as he laughed. 'Come!'

He beckoned to the children. He sat down on a stone nearby and rested his axe against it. He motioned for them to sit down opposite. The children came over and sat down on another stone, facing him. Arthur took off his rucksack and laid it down beside him. The whole scene was illuminated by the strange green light. Arthur felt a little less afraid and was the first to speak.

'Who were those strange women?' he asked.

'They are the Valkyries,' Thor replied. 'They are gone to the battle in far Araby. They are to choose those slain who are to feast with Odin in Valhalla. Their leader, Freya, will choose one half to feast with her in Folkvang.'

Arthur and Ginny thought of their father.

'Give the cup and the ring to my hand!' Thor commanded.

Arthur gave him the cup and Ginny took off the ring and handed it to him. He inspected them. Arthur spoke again. 'They look so ordinary,' he commented.

Thor held out the ring.

'You see this ring?' he stated. 'It was given to Queen Guinevere by the Lady of the Lake. It was forged by dwarfs, deep underground. It is indestructible.'

Thor held out the cup.

'This cup,' he continued, 'is the cup that from which drank Jesus Christ at the Last Supper and the Grail that King Arthur sought.'

He examined the cup and then went on.

'And as for the plainness of the cup, do you think that the Man, Who lived His life amongst thieves and outcasts and Who was born in a stable, would have truck with finery?'

Thor laughed. He threw his head back, and his whole body seemed to shake. He stopped laughing. 'How came you by these?' he asked, looking serious.

Ginny had relaxed a little, by now. 'We found some old rhymes in the library,' she answered. 'We think they were written by the original Leonard Dickinson.'

'Ah, Leonard Dickinson!' returned Thor. 'Let me tell you a tale.'

'Take these,' he directed, holding out the cup and the ring.

Thor gave the cup and the ring back to Arthur and Ginny. Ginny put the ring back on the third finger of her left hand, and Arthur put the cup in his rucksack. Thor leaned forward and put his hands on his knees. He started speaking conspiratorially to the children.

'Odin, my father, was so tired of the rash way I used my power, that, one day, while I was sleeping, he took my hammer away from me. He hid it on this Moor. He went in the guise of an old man with one eye and told Leonard Dickinson where he had hidden it. But I had seen. I went to Leonard Dickinson many times and in many guises, over the years, but I could not wrest the secret from him, even on his deathbed. Without my hammer, I am powerless!'

Thor shook his hand in the air. He then looked surprised.

'But I feel it near me!' he exclaimed.

'What have you got in that strange bag, Arthur?' he asked, pointing to the rucksack.

Arthur opened his rucksack and drew out the hammer. Thor grabbed it from Arthur.

'My hammer!' he cried joyfully.

Thor stood up, and, in one mighty movement, threw the hammer into the night sky. The children could see it circling up into the sky. It was a small, flickering light, high up. Arthur thought it looked like the satellite that he had seen previously. It then came back down to earth, giving out a whooshing noise. It returned to Thor's right hand, striking sparks from his gauntlet. Thor sat down, smiling.

'It is good to have Mjollnir to my hand again,' Thor said.

'Mjollnir?' queried Arthur.

'For that is the name of my hammer,' replied Thor.

He held out the hammer to Arthur.

'But, now you must take it!' he commanded.

'Us!' exclaimed Arthur, incredulously.

'Yes,' continued Thor, 'there is trouble in the town.'

'You mean, Albert Lockey?' asked Arthur.

'Lockey?' raged Thor. 'It is none other than Loki, my arch-enemy. He is up to his old tricks again.'

Thor stared at the children. 'He has not heard of the Cup and the Ring?' he queried.

'We think he has,' answered Arthur.

'Bones of Odin!' exclaimed Thor. 'Loki knows that he can gain great power from the possession of my hammer. He has been exiled from Asgard for many years, and that would not be so if he had the hammer. For that reason, it is of great import that you take the hammer.'

Thor held out the hammer to Arthur. He did not take it.

'Why can't you use your hammer against Loki?' he asked.

'Loki has been amongst men for many years,' Thor returned. 'He is familiar with their ways. I am not so familiar as you can tell by my speech.'

Thor shifted his weight on the stone.

'And despite my hammer', Thor continued, 'my power in this land is feeble. The gods of old are no longer remembered. New gods have come in their place. It is only by the worship of people such as the Dickinsons that my memory is kept alive. But there is an older magic. You must wake the giant.'

'Why us?' asked Arthur. It was getting late, it was cold up here, and he was thinking of his nice, warm bed.

Thor looked annoyed.

'That is the way the old magic is working,' he explained. 'It has chosen you two. Now, quickly, take the hammer. Take it, before I change my mind.'

Thor held out the hammer to Arthur once more. Arthur finally took it.

'And, now, you must take it to Ames Cliff!' Thor exhorted.

'Ames Cliff?' Arthur queried.

'You would call it Almscliff,' replied Thor. 'Loki will think that you will be going to the Cow and Calf, so you will be safe. At the next dawn, stand on the rock, and hold up the hammer. Remember, you must . . .'

Thor suddenly disappeared from the stone he had been sitting on. The green light snapped out. The railings and barbed wire sprouted up from the ground around the Swastika Stone as if they were things that were growing. Arthur and Ginny were grabbed from behind by rough hands.

CHAPTER ELEVEN

An Adventure in the Town Hall

The moon was shining down on the Swastika Stone. Six Policemen were standing around it. They were holding torches. Two of them had Arthur and Ginny in half nelsons. In the preceding scuffle, Arthur dropped the hammer on the ground. One of the Policemen picked it up. He was the Officer that the children knew well.

'Well done, lads,' he said. 'Albert Lockey said we would find these little beggars up here, and we did.'

He turned to the children.

'We're going to take you where you can't do any more harm', he said, 'deep under the town hall, Arthur and Guinevere!'

He laughed, savouring the moment. Ginny twisted in her captor's embrace, reached down with her mouth, and bit him hard in his arm. He let go of her, shaking his arm, wincing, and cursing. Ginny started running away, towards Heber's Ghyll. The Policemen began to follow. In the general confusion, Arthur was able to struggle free. He grabbed his rucksack and ran after Ginny. By the light of the moon, Arthur and Ginny stumbled down to the iron gate above Heber's Ghyll. It was very dark in the wood.

Going through the gate, they tumbled down the slippery path, slid down the bank of the beck, and hid under a bridge. A few moments later, there was the clatter of the Policemen's boots over the bridge. The sound receded down the Ghyll, then, a while later, the children heard the Policemen returning. There was shouting and the flashing of torches. They were searching the wood. There were comings and goings for about a half an hour. At one point, a torch shone under the bridge. The children huddled in the darkness. The beam of the torch moved around but did not pick them out. It moved on.

The children were getting cold. They were standing in the beck, and the water was soaking into their boots. Finally, the hue and cry died down, and the wood fell silent. Arthur and Ginny were just considering coming out of their hiding place, when they heard footsteps approaching. They recognised the voice of the Officer.

'Well, Tom,' he said, 'looks like they've got away.'

The other man said something.

'Oh,' said the Officer. 'Don't worry. We'll get them in the end.'

The other man said something else.

'I don't know,' answered the Officer. 'All I know is that Albert Lockey wants this worthless piece of iron in his office. I don't know why. He must be cracked. Anyway, there's a bottle of Scotch in there. Perhaps we'll try some. Eh, Tom?'

The men laughed, and their voices went off down the Ghyll. The children crept out from under the bridge. Arthur got out his flashlight. They sat down on a damp bench in the wood. Arthur had got a map out of his rucksack and was studying it.

'We've lost the hammer,' said Ginny, dejectedly. 'Why look at the map?'

'I've got a plan!' Arthur explained. 'I don't think we're quite done for, yet.'

Ginny listened to Arthur, all ears.

'Look, Ginny,' he said. 'I noticed that the hammer looks exactly like the one we saw Len and Molly with in the outhouse. If we can get that one, and, somehow, put it in the place of the real one in the town hall, then we might just fool Albert Lockey, I mean Loki.'

'But, how do we get to Almscliff Crag after that?' asked Ginny. 'We can't walk all the way. It's miles from here.'

'I've thought of that as well,' said Arthur. 'We'll get there by bus!'

He reached into a pocket of his Cagjack and got out a bus timetable.

'Where did you get that?' queried Ginny.

'I got it in the library on Saturday,' Arthur replied. 'I thought it might turn out useful.'

Arthur studied the timetable and then looked at his watch.

'It's nine thirty', he said, 'and the last bus to Harrogate leaves at about eleven thirty. We'll have plenty of time to swap the hammers and catch the bus. I think that bus will go through some of the villages near Almscliff Crag.'

'Arthur,' said Ginny, 'I don't like to say this, but wouldn't it be easier to tell Len and Molly? They could take us to the crag in their trap.'

'I've been thinking about that,' answered Arthur. 'Do you really think they'd believe us? And, what if they tell the Police? Besides, you heard what Thor said. The magic has chosen us. I think it would be better if we did the whole thing by ourselves.'

'I suppose you're right,' said Ginny. 'I was rather hoping that the cup and the ring might be able to help us.'

'They might still help us,' returned Arthur. 'But we don't really know what they can do. I think they were a kind of key to help us find the hammer. Now, the most important thing is to get the hammer to Almscliff Crag. First we'll rest here for a bit.'

Arthur had a bit of Kendal Mint Cake left in his rucksack. The children shared it. There was no drink left. Finally, Arthur stood up. 'Well,' he said, 'we'd better go back to the farm and find the other hammer.'

Arthur put the map back in the rucksack, put the timetable in his pocket, and they set off, Arthur lighting the way with his flashlight. The moon was shining through gaps in the trees, making the water of the beck seem phosphorescent. They approached the road at the bottom of Heber's Ghyll with caution. There was nobody about. They went along the road, up the track to the farm, and into the farmyard. There was a Police car in the farmyard. They dived for cover. They realised that there was no one in the farmyard, not even Jess, so they made their way inquisitively over to the living room window. The curtains were not drawn. They peeped inside. Len and Molly were visible, sitting on the settee in their nightclothes and holding hands. They looked small and helpless. Over them towered two Policemen. One was the Officer. The children could hear what he was saying.

'. . . foolish of you to deny that two children were living here. They have been making a great deal of trouble on the Moor, you know that?'

Leonard said something in a low voice.

'I don't care about that,' boomed the Officer. 'All I know is that we need to question them. Your duty now is to tell us if they come back here. You understand?'

Leonard replied, but the children could still not hear what he was saying. The Officer answered Leonard.

'I don't like your attitude, Mr Dickinson. Any more of that and we'll have you all down the nick. Anyway, as I think you would say, I'm a busy man, and I've plenty of things to do, so we'll say goodnight.'

The Policemen made motions to leave. The children ducked down below the window sill and quickly crept doubled-up to the outhouse. It was locked. They ran up the steps, and the door at the top was open. They hid on the half landing. They heard the sound of boots on the cobbles, doors slamming, and the Police car driving away.

'Well,' observed Arthur, 'we can't tell Len and Molly now.'

Arthur moved the feeble beam of the flashlight across the walls of the outhouse. It shone on the false hammer. Ginny went down the stairs inside and took it off the wall. It was held up with only two nails. She took it back to Arthur who put it in his rucksack. The children crept back through the door, down the steps, and set off into town.

They decided to make their way into town by the backstreets. There was street lighting here, so Arthur turned off his flashlight to conserve the batteries. They were just going past St Margaret's Church, when they heard a car coming. They hid in the snicket by the old stones. A Police car roared past. The stones looked black and threatening. They realised why no one wanted to come here at night.

Eventually, Arthur and Ginny managed to get to the back of the town hall without being noticed. They found an iron gate guarding the entrance to a small courtyard. The gate was padlocked. They climbed over it with some difficulty. Builders had been working on the roof, and there was scaffolding reaching up to it from the courtyard. Arthur climbed on to the scaffolding and examined a ground-floor window. He was trying to see if there was any kind of alarm. He could not see anything, so he dug his nails into the gap between the frame and window and tugged. Surprisingly, the window came open easily. Someone had not locked it. Arthur listened. No alarm had gone off. He breathed a sigh of relief.

Arthur got through the window into a small office. He turned on his flashlight. Ginny climbed on to the scaffolding, and Arthur helped her through the window. They found a door out of the office into a corridor. Ginny tried the handle. The door was locked. Ginny looked around the office. She saw a filing cabinet with a bunch of keys hanging on a string by its side. She took the keys.

'Could these be the keys to the door, Arthur?' she asked, whispering.

Arthur tried each key in the door, while Ginny held the flashlight. He fumbled with the keys for some time. It seemed that the very last one that he tried opened the door. They left the keys on a desk and went out into the corridor. Up some steps to the right was the entrance hall. The children went up into the entrance hall and then turned up the stairs. They reached the landing and found Loki's office. Ginny tried the door. It was locked. They looked around, but could find no key. They were wondering what to do, when they heard footsteps on the stairs. Arthur saw a broom cupboard opposite to Loki's office.

'In this cupboard!' said Arthur in a low voice.

Arthur shoved Ginny into the cupboard and then followed himself, turning off his flashlight. He shut the door to the cupboard. They heard the footsteps approach, a key turning in the lock of the office, and someone entering it. The children waited a bit, then Arthur cracked the door open. Through the glass panel in the door to the office, Arthur could see Loki sitting at the desk. He was unaware of the cupboard door's opening. He seemed preoccupied.

'It's Loki!' he whispered to Ginny.

Arthur waited for a while and then peered out again. Loki had got the hammer in his hands. He had put on a black cloak and was intoning something over the hammer in a strange voice. His voice got louder and louder. He put the hammer on the desk and held his hands apart over it. As he continued chanting, a blue flame appeared between his forefingers. The flame crackled and spat and there was a smell of electrical burning in the air.

Loki moved the flame over the hammer. There was no reaction from it. Loki tried the same thing again. The electric arc struck up between his fingers, and he moved it over the hammer. There was still there was no reaction from the hammer. He looked angry and shook his fist at it. Finally, Loki took some keys out from under a flowerpot on the window ledge, put the hammer in a drawer in the desk, and locked the drawer. He put the keys back under the flowerpot. He took of his cloak and hung it up in a steel cabinet. He sat for some time with his elbow on the desk and his fingers against his cheek, pondering. He drummed the fingers of his other hand on the desk. Eventually, he got up to go out. Arthur ducked back into the cupboard. Loki's footsteps could be heard, going out of the office, along the landing, and descending the stairs. The children waited in the cupboard until they could hear no more sounds.

'What did you see?' Ginny asked Arthur.

'I've seen where the hammer is!' answered Arthur.

Arthur and Ginny crept out of the cupboard. Ginny tried the handle of Loki's office. The door was unlocked. Loki had apparently forgotten to lock it. Arthur and Ginny went into the office, turning on the light, and Arthur retrieved the keys for the desk from under the flowerpot. He unlocked the drawer and got out the hammer. He got out the false hammer from his rucksack. He put them on the desk and compared them. They looked identical. Arthur put the false hammer in the drawer, closed it, locked it, and put the keys back under the flowerpot. Then, he took the real hammer from the top of the desk and stowed it away in his rucksack. The children were just making sure that nothing had been disturbed, when they heard footsteps on the stairs again. Arthur recognised the fall of the feet.

'It's Loki again!' he whispered.

Arthur and Ginny rushed out of the office, making certain to turn off the light and close the door. They bundled once more into the broom cupboard. They heard the footsteps approach, the key turn in the lock of the office, and the footsteps recede again. Loki had come back to lock the office. The children waited for another age until they thought no one was about. They came out and made their way down the stairs to the front doors of the town hall. They were on a latch, and the children easily opened them from inside. They came out into the street. The last bus to Harrogate was pulling out of the bus station. The children ran down the street after the bus, shouting and waving, but the driver appeared not to take any notice. The bus drove down Brook Street and off into the night. They were stranded in Ilkley.

CHAPTER TWELVE

The Journey to Almscliff

The streets of Ilkley were deserted. Arthur and Ginny were walking down Brook Street. In the window display of a clothes shop, the sightless eyes of mannequins looked down with vacant stares. The traffic lights at the bottom of Brook Street turned green and echoes slipped silently past the lights on their way to non-existent places. Rats scurried in cellars.

'That's blown it!' said Arthur.

'Looks like it', replied Ginny, 'but we'll just look down here and see what we can see.'

They entered a maze of backstreets behind the station.

'Wait a minute!' said Arthur. 'I think I remember there's a bike shop around here somewhere. Perhaps we can nick some bikes.'

'Don't be silly,' answered Ginny. 'They'll be locked well away by now. Anyway, should we really do that?'

'Anything, if it gets us to Almscliff Crag,' replied Arthur.

They were walking down a street of terraced houses. They passed one in particular and spotted two racing bikes leaning up against a fence. The door of the house was open. Arthur went over and examined the bikes.

'They're unlocked!' whispered Arthur. 'Quick, Ginny, grab this!'

He seized one of the bikes, wheeled it over to Ginny, and tried to thrust it into her hands. She held back.

'Put it back!' she exclaimed, pushing the bike away from her. 'You'll get us into all sorts of trouble.'

'Look, Ginny,' said Arthur, getting annoyed. 'We've got to get to Almscliff Crag. Right?'

Ginny slowly nodded her head.

'Then this is the only way we'll get there,' Arthur continued, pushing the bike back into Ginny's hands.

Ginny finally made up her mind. She decided that they would have to steal the bikes. She accepted the bike from Arthur. Arthur quickly got the other bike. Arthur and Ginny set off on the bikes as quietly as they could. An athletic-looking man stepped out of the house, saw that his bikes were gone, and dashed out into the street. He spotted Arthur and Ginny pedalling away.

'Oy! You! Coom back!' he shouted.

It was the runner from the Moor. He had got home and was planning to go on a midnight cycle ride with his girlfriend. He began to run after the children. He was still dressed in his tracksuit and trainers and was able to keep up with the children. They pedalled furiously in high gear and were only able to shake him off after a half a mile. He stood in the road near the gasworks, shaking his fist at them and cursing. They were worn out after that and cycled along slowly. They were travelling along the Leeds road below Ben Rhydding. Arthur motioned for them to stop. He got out a map and looked at it in the beam of his flashlight.

'Best if we go to Almscliff Crag by the backroads,' he suggested. 'We go over a bridge at the bottom of Ben Rhydding. Then we turn right and follow on from there.'

The children discovered that the bikes had lights. They turned them on and carried on. The last house lights in Ben Rhydding were clicking off. The wind was increasing. The children turned over a small suspension bridge and cycled across. The water of the Wharfe slithered darkly past below. There were no street lights beyond. They set off into the darkness. After a gradual climb, they passed through Askwith. The village was dead. An inn sign squeaked mournfully in the wind. They began to go downhill, towards Weston. From a wood, they heard the repeated bark of a fox. They went past Weston Hall. The twisted branches of trees moved in the breeze, as if they were trying to reach out and grasp them. They reached the main road at Otley, which went down a hill to the right. Arthur looked at the map again.

'We turn left just down there, then up to Farnley,' he said, pointing.

They cycled silently through the outskirts of Otley, looking out for any Police cars. It was long past pub-closing time, and there was no one about. Bathed in the antiseptic street lighting, the litter chased itself around in skittish circles. The children made their way up a long, steep hill on the far side of Otley. They had to get off their bikes and walk at one stage. They passed the last of the street lamps and went on into the darkness. Night birds screeched from a dark wood nearby.

They had just turned left towards Farnley, when they heard a car approaching. They stopped and listened. It was turning towards Farnley. There was the gate to a field nearby. Arthur spotted the gate. It was padlocked. He lugged the bikes quickly over the gate. The children climbed over, put the bikes behind a wall by the gate, and turned off the lights. They crouched behind the wall and waited. The car came up to the gate, slowed down, and stopped, the engine running. Whoever it was, they were looking for something. The car drove off again, its headlamps blazing.

The children waited for a while and then got their bikes back on the road and turned the lights on again. They arrived at Farnley and turned down a hill. They were zooming along beside a wood adjacent to a reservoir. They turned very quickly around a corner before a bridge. There was a Police roadblock on the bridge. Arthur and Ginny could not stop in time. They cycled straight into the arms of the waiting Police.

The Officer was there. He had got hold of Ginny. Another Policeman was holding Arthur. The children's bikes lay abandoned.

'What have we here?' said the Officer, sarcastically. 'Out for a night bike-ride, are we?'

Ginny reached down with her mouth and tried to bite him in the arm. He pulled her arm up more tightly behind her back.

'Oh, no, little Missy!' the Officer sneered. 'We don't try that again!'

Ginny kicked him in the shins. He flinched but still held on to Ginny. The Policemen bundled Arthur and Ginny into a car. They put the bikes into another. They set off towards Otley.

In the front of the children's car, the Policemen had the radio on and were chatting. There was a plastic partition between them and the children. Ginny noticed that the Policemen had not locked the door nearest to her. Arthur's rucksack was beside her. Ginny thought quickly. She reached into the rucksack and found the hammer. She waited until they were slowing down around a corner, opened the door, and threw herself out. Her fall was broken by some soft mud in a ditch. The door clicked shut behind her, and the Police car sped on into the night. The Policemen had not noticed. She lay panting in the ditch. She was a bit bruised and cut, but she was free.

Almscliff Crag

The moon had set. Ginny stumbled towards Almscliff Crag in the darkness. She vaguely knew the way, and there was some light in the sky from the big cities nearby. Eventually she saw the black shape of the crag against the sky and made her way towards it. She reached a footpath sign pointing over a field and went up the field to the crag. It towered over her. It had a big cleft down the middle of it. Ginny went up into the cleft. The rock of the crag was in twisted layers. Ginny went over a concrete wall between the two halves of the crag, and managed to get up on to the crag from behind. She got to the top of the crag, sat down on it, and waited for dawn.

There was a light shower of rain towards dawn. Ginny did not feel at all wet. She did not feel tired, thirsty, or hungry. Instead, she felt comfortable and warm. She looked down at her left hand. The ring felt warm on her finger. It was the ring that was helping her, she decided.

Ginny could see the lights of Otley twinkling in the valley and a line of lights reaching up the Chevin on the far side. She could see the sky lightening in the east. She got up from the rock and stood holding the hammer in her right hand. Just as the sun came over the horizon, she held the hammer up high. She waited. Nothing happened.

'What was Thor trying to tell us at the Swastika Stone?' thought Ginny.

Ginny could hear a low humming noise. She looked at the hammer. The noise was coming from the hammer. The ornate decoration on the hammer was beginning to glow. Ginny studied the decoration. It seemed to be rearranging itself. She could make out words. She read them.

AT THIS VERY TIME OF YEAR, MAIDEN, THROW ME TO THE AIR

Ginny knew what to do. She gathered all her strength and threw the hammer high up into the air, just as Thor had done. The hammer spiralled into the sky, glinting in the light, and then returned whooshing to her hand. It cut her hand. Suddenly, there was a crashing peal of thunder, and a searing bolt of blue lightning struck the crag, only some feet from where Ginny was standing. She threw herself to one side on to the rock. Lying on her stomach, she looked out over the Vale of York. A gigantic figure was striding across the vale. It was the giant.

Ginny could not make out what the giant was wearing. The giant was only a dark, shadowy shape. Ginny could see the rising sun shining through the shape. Ginny got up from the rock. She heard a noise behind her. She whirled around. The Police were coming up the field below the crag. They had seen Ginny as her body was silhouetted against the sky. The giant gradually drew near to the crag. A Policeman was climbing on to the rock below Ginny. The giant stepped over the crag. At that point, Ginny was carried aloft by a huge gust of wind.

CHAPTER THIRTEEN

The Giant Walks

The Police car was travelling along the Leeds Road out of Otley. It was dark, now that the moon had set. The instrumentation on the dashboard of the Police car was glowing fiercely. Arthur was trying not to draw attention to himself. He hoped that the Policemen would not notice that Ginny was missing. The Police car went over a pothole in the road and lurched. The Policeman in the front passenger seat glanced back to make sure the children were all right. He spotted that Ginny was not in her seat. He craned quickly around and checked the backseat. He shook the Officer in the driver's seat by the shoulder.

"Ere', he said, 'that girl's missing!'

'What!' exclaimed the Officer. 'Has that little minx got away?'

The Police car pulled to a halt, the brakes squealing. The Policemen got out and inspected the backseat. They saw that Ginny had gone. They dragged Arthur out of the car, threw him against the body of the car, and shook him.

'Where is the little lady?' shouted the Officer.

'I don't know!' wailed Arthur.

The Officer shook him.

'You must know something,' he barked. 'Tell me where she is, or so help me . . .'

The Officer raised his arm to strike Arthur. Arthur broke down, crying.

'She's back on the road near Farnley,' he sobbed.

The Policemen roughly shoved Arthur into the car, turned it around, and took off towards Farnley.

When they had got close to Farnley, the Policemen drove very slowly along, looking around. From time to time they stopped at gates and looked over. They drove as far as the Harrogate Road, but found nothing.

'It's no good, Tom,' said the Officer. 'We could be searching for hours in the dark, looking for her.'

'Well,' said the other Officer, 'at least we've got one of them. Let's give up, Col, and take this one back to Albert Lockey. We'll call out some more of the lads.'

The Officer agreed, turned the car around, and they headed towards Ilkley. Arthur was glad that they had not found Ginny but was a little bit apprehensive about what would happen next.

The Police car arrived at Ilkley town hall. Arthur grabbed hold of his rucksack and put it on his back. The Policemen manhandled Arthur up to Loki's office. Arthur was too tired to struggle. Loki was waiting in the office. He was visible through the glass, drumming his fingers on the desk and resting his head in his other hand. He obviously knew that the Police had found Arthur and was waiting. The Policemen pushed Arthur through the door. Loki told them to wait outside. He stood up behind the desk.

'You know you're wanted for some very serious offences?' he said sternly.

'I don't know. What?' asked Arthur, boldly.

'You know very well,' Loki said.

Loki started counting on his fingers.

'One. Taking archaeological remains from the Moor. Two. Evading arrest. Three. Stealing bicycles. It's a wonder I don't throw you straight in the nick.'

Loki stared at Arthur. 'Where is your sister?' he demanded, striking the desk.

Arthur thought quickly.

'She's on her way to Harrogate,' he blurted.

'And why is she going there?' Loki raged.

'She's going to tell the Police at Harrogate. We know all about you, you scumbag!' Arthur spouted, hardly realising what he was saying.

In one swift movement, Loki came out from behind the desk and tried to strike Arthur. But something strange happened. Loki's body locked. He tried to hit Arthur, but his body was rigid. Arthur felt a warmth in the pit of his back. The cup was in his rucksack. Arthur realised that it was the cup protecting him. Loki fell back against the desk, panting.

'And what do you know about me, Arthur?' sneered Loki.

Arthur thought quickly again. He did not think that it was a good idea to tell Loki exactly what he knew.

'You're in league with big business,' he said, measuring his words. 'I bet they stand to make a lot of money out of Ilkley, and I bet you won't go short either.'

Loki had recovered. He went behind the desk and leaned on it.

'What if that's true?' he scoffed. 'What are a puny couple of kids going to do about it?'

'Just wait till the Harrogate Police hear about this,' Arthur replied bravely. 'They'll soon sort you out.'

'Your sister won't even get that far,' Loki snorted. 'I've got some of my men out looking for her at this very moment.'

Loki got the keys for the desk out from under the flowerpot, unlocked the drawer with the false hammer in it, and drew it out.

'You know what this is, don't you, Arthur?' he asked, waving the hammer under Arthur's nose.

'Yes. It's a worthless bit of iron we found on the Moor,' replied Arthur, lying.

'It may look like that to you. To me, it is my passport to Asgard,' he said, laughing and kissing the false hammer.

He put the false hammer in a briefcase, which he picked up.

'And now,' he said, 'we're going up to the Cow and Calf, but I'm taking you along with me in case your sister tries any dirty tricks.'

Loki called the two Policemen in from outside. Under Loki's direction, they tied Arthur's hands in front of him and pushed him downstairs. The cup did not help him. Outside, there was a squad of Police cars gathered. Arthur was bundled into one of the cars. Loki got into another and a convoy drove up to the Cow and Calf. They pulled up and waited below the rocks. There was a long pause in which nothing much happened. Some of the Policemen got out of the cars, lit cigarettes, and chatted.

Eventually, the sky grew lighter in the east. It began to rain. Loki looked at his watch and got out of the car he had been in, putting on a raincoat. He opened his briefcase and got out the false hammer. Then, he strode up towards the Cow Rock, smiling grimly and holding the hammer in his hand.

'What's Albert Lockey up to?' said one Policeman in Arthur's car.

'I'm not sure,' said the Officer. 'All I know is to obey orders.'

Loki appeared at the top of the Cow Rock. The first sliver of the sun was appearing over the horizon. Loki held up the false hammer. He was mouthing some sort of spell. He stood there for some time. Arthur looked to the east. He could see something. A gigantic figure was strolling up the Wharfe valley. Arthur was ecstatic. He knew that it was the giant and that Ginny had wakened him. The Policemen took no notice.

As the figure drew nearer, Arthur spotted a smaller figure flying through the air, apparently on its shoulder. Arthur recognised that it was Ginny. Still the Policemen took no notice. Arthur began to realise that only he could see the Giant because of the cup he had with him. The giant drew up to the Cow Rock. Loki was at the height of his invocations. He also did not seem to notice the giant. The giant stepped over the Cow Rock, stumbling a little. Loki was suddenly raised into the air by a huge gust of wind, which then let go of him. He fell down the cliff, screaming. He tumbled on to a large rock at the bottom, which broke his back. The same gust of wind deposited Ginny neatly and gently on top of the Cow Rock. The giant strode off to the west.

Arthur caught a movement. To the south, another giant figure was approaching. It looked to be female this time and seemed to have a long, flowing skirt, in which it was carrying something. The figure stepped over the ridge to the south and let go of its skirt. A deluge of large boulders came tumbling out of the sky. They hit the Police cars with loud thumps and many of the tops caved in. The top of Arthur's car went in with a crash and it hit the Officer. His head fractured. He slumped in his seat, bleeding. At the same time, the car door next to Arthur was flung open by the shock. Arthur crawled out as best he could with his bound hands. The scene was a shambles. There were dead and injured Policemen lying everywhere. Some were trying to help others.

Arthur heard the sound of pounding hoofs. He saw a man with a red beard mounted on a jet-black horse galloping down the ridge to the south. It was Thor. He had been wakened from the Swastika Stone. He was followed by the Valkyries on their horses. Their blonde hair flowed in the breeze. Thor charged down the slope, spotted Arthur, and came over to him.

'Well, Arthur,' he cried, 'the maiden has awakened the giant, as the soothsayer Leonard Dickinson foretold!'

'I think it's wonderful!' exclaimed Arthur. 'But how do you know about the Dickinson family rhyme?'

'I know many things,' said Thor and laughed. 'Am I not a god?'

Arthur nodded and held up his bonds.

'Could you get me free?' he asked Thor.

Thor got out his axe, and with one swipe between Arthur's hands, the rope was cut. Arthur immediately ran up the rise to the Cow Rock. Ginny was still standing on the Cow Rock, looking very dazed. Arthur grabbed hold of Ginny's hand. He could see that she was holding the hammer in her other hand.

'Are you all right, Ginny?' Arthur asked.

'Yeees,' Ginny answered weakly.

Thor and the Valkyries were harrying the remaining Policemen. Thor's axe and Valkyries' spears shone in the light as they slashed at the men. The Policemen were running away. Finally, when all the Policemen had been routed, Thor rode up the steep slope to the Cow Rock. The Valkyries followed and came to a halt behind him. Thor came over to the children on his horse. He was level with the part of the Cow Rock that the children were standing on.

'Well met!' roared Thor. 'I see that you still have the hammer, Guinevere. Give it to my hand.'

Ginny was recovering. She handed the hammer to Thor. He looked at it in his hand.

'Ah!' he cried. 'It is good to have my hammer again, after so many years!'

He threw the hammer high into the air. It seemed to tumble in the air, defying gravity, and then returned with a rush of air to his hand.

Arthur still had questions. 'So Loki is dead?' he asked.

'That is only his earthly form,' replied Thor. 'He will return, no doubt, to make trouble again.'

'Will we ever see you again?' queried Arthur.

'There is a time coming, and I fear it will not be long hence, when I must do battle upon the plains of Vigrid at Ragnarok,' Thor answered. 'But for now, I have the hammer, and I will return to my palace of Belskirnir in Asgard. I may not return to earth for many's the year, if at all.'

Thor saw the children's sad faces. He smiled and turned to Ginny.

'What have you got on your left hand, Guinevere?' he asked.

Ginny held up her hand. 'The Ring!' she said.

Thor turned to Arthur. 'And what have you got in your bag, Arthur?' he queried.

Arthur took off his rucksack, rummaged in it, and pulled out the cup. He held it up to Thor. 'The cup!' Arthur said.

Thor smiled more broadly as he looked at the children.

'Remember, you still have the cup and the ring. They will guard you in all the things that may befall you in the times that are to come, even if I am not here. Now, Freya has something for you.'

The beautiful woman leading the Valkyries moved her horse forward.

'Take this, children,' she said in a voice that rang like bells.

She held out her hunting horn. Ginny took it.

'Wind upon it when all seems lost,' she said.

The children thanked Freya.

Thor turned to Ginny. 'Now, Guinevere,' Thor said, softly, kissing her.

Thor turned to Arthur. 'Now, Arthur,' he boomed, grasping Arthur's hands in both of his and then clapping him on the back.

'We must be gone!' thundered Thor. 'Remember this day. Farewell, Arthur and Guinevere!'

Thor turned his horse around. He signalled to the Valkyries. They wheeled around and thundered off with Thor to the south-west and along Rocky Valley. Thor's arm was raised in salute to the children. Arthur and Ginny waved to him until he had disappeared.

The children turned towards the town. It was basking in the light of the morning sun. It seemed that the whole of Ilkley was theirs. They went over to the edge of the Cow Rock. Far below was Loki's body. There was still some movement in it. His hand moved, fell on the ground, and opened. Instead of the false hammer falling out, a pure white dove fluttered into the air and flew across the face of the Cow Rock.

CHAPTER FOURTEEN

Aftermath

'And where the 'ell do you think you've bin?' raged Leonard, his face red.

Arthur and Ginny had returned home only to be greeted by an enraged Leonard and Molly. Leonard had cornered the children in the living room. Molly was standing by his side, looking grim.

'We've been up at the Cow and Calf,' said Arthur in a tremulous voice, wringing his hands.

'Oh, have you now!' stormed Leonard. 'What do you mean by staying out all neet and mecking Molly and me 'alf sick wi' woorry? You know t' Police were lookin' for you?'

'We had to be up at the Cow and Calf,' explained Arthur.

Leonard ignored Arthur.

'An' anoother thing', he fumed, 'where are your bikes? An' there's a bottle of me wine missin'. Have you bin drinkin' on t' Moor?'

'Thor was up at the Cow and Calf!' wailed Arthur.

A complete change came over Leonard. His face altered from anger to an expression with a mixture of surprise and joy.

'You mean our Thor? The Thor?' he whooped, grabbing hold of Molly.

'Yes,' returned Arthur, 'he chased the Police away and got his hammer back. He was sleeping under the Swastika Stone.'

'Oooh!' Leonard gushed 'I felt his presence at this farm. I knew our worship was not in vain.'

Leonard bent down and slapped his knees. He stood up, recovering.

'Rum doin's oop at t' Cow and Calf,' he said. 'The way I 'eard, it were that the Police were tryin' to stop Albert Lockey throwin' 'imself of t' Cow. There were a landslip and 'e was knocked off. A man and some women were out ridin' and their 'orses went berserk.'

Leonard looked long at Arthur and Ginny. 'What were you doin' in all this?' he queried.

There seemed little point in keeping everything a secret now. Between them, Arthur and Ginny told Leonard and Molly about all the adventures that they had had. At the end, Leonard scratched his head.

'Well!' he exclaimed. 'Soom people may think it queer we worship Thor, so I don't find your story at all strange!'

He turned to Molly. 'Now, look at these bairns!' he scolded. 'They're tired an' 'ungry. Get us soom breakfast, Moother!'

Molly scurried into the kitchen. She soon made breakfast. There was toast, cereal, tea, coffee, milk, marmalade, and butter. Arthur and Ginny felt as if they could eat it all. Molly was surprised at their change in appetite. During breakfast, there was a phone call. Leonard answered it. He came back to the table, smiling.

'Fantastic news!' he exclaimed. ''Ang on to your 'ats. Leonora has joost rung. She says she's 'eard that your Dad is to be released.'

'I don't believe you!' cried Arthur.

'It's true!' whooped Leonard.

Ginny was ecstatic. 'Dad is free! Dad is free!' she shouted, waving her hands in the air. She stopped. 'Does this mean we're going home?' she asked.

'Nay, lass,' explained Leonard. 'Your moother thinks you should stay oop 'ere for t' present. She doesn't want to interrupt your education.'

'Then we can still go up on the Moor!' Ginny exclaimed.

'Joost as long as you don't stay out all neet agen!' said Leonard. 'I joost wondered what t' local radio 'as to say about all the things 'appening at t' Cow and Calf.'

Leonard went over and turned on the radio. Deep groaning noises came from it as the valves warmed up. Then they heard the following:

'... Albert Lockey, the Ilkley town mayor threw himself off the famous Cow and Calf rocks on the edge of Ilkley Moor this morning in an apparent suicide bid. He was dead on arrival at hospital. As a result of his death, it has transpired that there was considerable corruption in the Ilkley Police force. Pending an investigation, the entire force has been suspended.

And now a round up of international news . . .'

Arthur and Ginny smiled at each other. Folfoot Farm and the Moor were safe. They carried on with their breakfast. Then their ears pricked up again. They heard on the radio that,

'The two British airmen held by Sheikh Ranish are to be handed over to UN officials at midday today. Sheikh Ranish made a broadcast this morning. He said that he had had a dream in which Allah had told him to release the airmen . . .'

'I always said that he was a madman,' said Arthur, rejoicing. 'But at least he's let our Dad go.'

The radio continued,

'. . . could last one hundred years. Over to our Science Correspondent.

The continuing problems in the Middle East and the tailing off of North Sea oil-production meant that the Government was obliged to introduce petrol rationing in the spring. For some time now, it has been suspected that there might be vast oil reserves lying untapped in the Western Approaches. It was announced this morning that, as a result of extensive surveying, a giant oilfield has been discovered off south-west England. The new oilfield has the potential of supplying whole of the needs of the UK for oil for at least the next one hundred years . . .'

Arthur and Ginny joined hands and waltzed around the living room.

Ginny looked puzzled. 'Arthur?' she said. 'Something strange is happening. Everything is coming right. Could it be the giant and the hammer?'

'You're darned right!' exclaimed Arthur. 'The old magic is working!'

The radio went on.

'. . . In a surprise move the Government admitted that provision for the controversial scheme of Care in the Community for mentally ill people was not adequate. There has been increasing concern about the number of people having nowhere to go and sleeping rough. The prime minister announced this morning that, in certain areas, the smaller mental hospitals would be reopened for the present. This was, he said, to allow a breathing space in which more appropriate measures could be introduced . . .'

Arthur and Ginny continued waltzing. Jim would have somewhere to go where people would understand him. The radio still continued,

'. . . A breakthrough in the treatment of rheumatoid arthritis has been announced from the States. A new drug, Phembrutol, has been discovered that, in trials, considerably alleviated the effects of arthritis. Researchers are already hailing it as a miracle drug in the prevention and treatment of arthritis. If the clinical trials are successful, the drug could be on prescription in the UK within the next year . . .'

Arthur and Ginny ran out into the farmyard, laughing. Mum would be cured of her arthritis. Everything was wonderful. They giggled and sang for the rest of the morning.

The children's father was released at midday on that Thursday. He was none the worse for his ordeal, but he rested at home for a while on his return to Britain. Eventually, the children had a tearful reunion with him when he visited Ilkley a few weeks later.

On the Friday after their adventures, Arthur and Ginny explained to Leonard how and where they had left their bikes. They went out in the trap and found them still near the Doubler Stones. The bikes were a bit rusty from having been outside in the rain, but were serviceable. The children rode them back to Folfoot Farm. Arthur and Ginny began at Ilkley Grammar the next Monday. From the beginning, Ginny excelled at everything she did, but especially in music and art. She almost seemed to be one step ahead of her teachers. Some people thought she was a genius, but Arthur knew that it was the Ring that she always wore on her finger. Arthur went rock climbing at the Cow and Calf Quarry and in Rocky Valley and contented himself with not doing nearly as well as Ginny in class. He used his dowsing rods only once again. Neither did he need his drugs. Whenever he felt a turn coming on, he would drink from the cup and a feeling of peace would fill his whole body.

The children forgave Alison Green for betraying them to Albert Lockey. She admitted that she had been infatuated with him and since his death she could not see why. The children did not explain that it probably had been some sort of magic. They were often up on the Moor with Alison and sometimes met Joe Grimshaw there.

For the present, as weeks turned into months, the children almost forgot about their adventures. However, on stormy nights the children would look up from Folfoot Farm to the lightning flickering around the Swastika Stone and would remember.

One, Two, Three, Four,
The Stones they stand upon the Moor,
The Hammer it is lost to Thor,
They all await the Maiden pure.

Explanations, Acknowledgements, Apologies, and Supplications

Some things need to be said about this book, if only to thank various people for their help.

The facts concerning the Moor and Ilkley have been kept to faithfully and have only been bent a little in places to suit the story. In particular, Folfoot Farm does not exist. All the people in the story are fictitious, apart from The Captain and Jim. The Captain lives in Ben Rhydding. His calculation was actually performed. Jim now lives in Thackley, but he was once in the local mental hospital. The patients of that hospital are not camping out on the Moor, yet. I should mention that the Ilkley Police carry out their duties admirably, so far as I am aware, and are not in league with the town mayor. There is not, in fact, a mayor in Ilkley.

My thanks go to Ilkley Tourist Information, Ilkley Library, the Manor House Museum, and Ilkley Gazette for helping me with details.

I should like also to thank numerous people for encouragement and advice, particularly Keith Allden, a geologist friend of mine, and Clare Bevan, the authoress.

My thanks also go to Alan and Griselda Garner for allowing me to use some of Alan's ideas. I recommend *The Weirdstone of Brisingamen*, *The Moon of Gomrath*, *Elidor*, and *The Owl Service*, amongst many others, by Alan Garner.

I apologise if some of the places in this book were not described in full or for anything that I may have left out. I could not go into too much detail, for fear of boring readers unfamiliar with Wharfedale. Equally well, the descriptions are only my opinion. I hope they do not offend anyone.

The Yorkshire dialect has been rendered as well as it could be without making it unreadable. I have generally left out the thee's and thou's. It will seem a little twee to a true speaker. I apologise if I have left out or misused any dialect words, but the whole text was checked by a Yorkshireman!

The Moor and Wharfedale are there to be enjoyed. If you go up on the Moor, follow the Countryside Code. Please take sensible footwear and adequate clothing with you and leave the plants, insects, and wildlife for others to enjoy. Take your litter home with you. And, please, I beg you, leave the stones I have described, alone. There already is a railing around the Swastika Stone to stop vandals. People carve their names into the Cow Rock almost daily, it seems. The stones were there long before you and will be there long after you have gone. It would be stupid to destroy the record of thousands of years ago with one mindless act of vandalism. If the stones are left alone, we might, one day, find out what the markings on them mean. You might even find out. Good luck!

Martin Kendall Ilkley as of February 1993